KINDRED SPIRITS

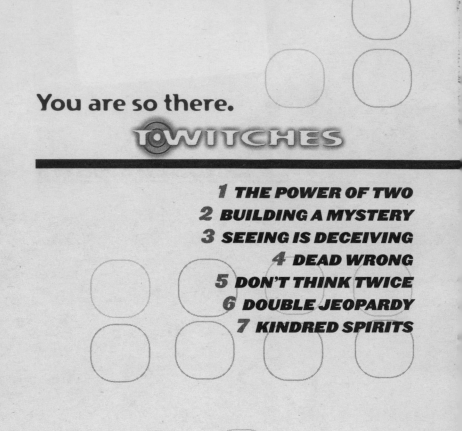

You are so there.

T*WITCHES

T*WITCHES

H.B. GILMOUR
& RANDI REISFELD

SCHOLASTIC INC.
NEW YORK TORONTO LONDON AUCKLAND SYDNEY
MEXICO CITY NEW DELHI HONG KONG BUENOS AIRES

ISBN 0-439-47219-9

12 11 10 9 8 7 6 5 4 3 2 1   3 4 5 6 7 8/0

Printed in the U.S.A.   40
First Scholastic printing, February 2003

DEDICATION

For Fred and Harry, kindred spirits, indeed.
—H.B.G.

This book is for a true kindred spirit, Bethany Buck,
who did not fail and did not falter, all the while
enduring an entire season in backbreaking pain.
She, as much as anyone, contributed to this book.

I could say all the good ideas were hers, but hey,
there's a limit to my generosity. Fortunately,
there's no such quota on hers.
Thanx, BB—be BACK soon!
—R.R.

KINDRED SPIRITS

CHAPTER ONE
JOURNEY TO COVENTRY

Karsh, the wise warlock who'd known and protected them all their lives, was dead.

Ileana, their guardian witch, was weak with grief.

Miranda, the birth mother they'd met only weeks before, was dependent on their dangerous, untrustworthy uncle.

They had no one to rely on now but each other.

They were leaving all that was safe and familiar to travel to a tiny island of witches and warlocks, most of them strangers . . . and a few who wanted them dead.

These were the facts obsessing fifteen-year-old Camryn Barnes, messing with her mind as she headed for the airport snack shop to buy mints for herself and gum for her sister, Alex.

It was 5:45 A.M. Their flight to Wisconsin, the first leg of their journey to Coventry Island, would board in less than fifteen minutes. And aside from wanting gum — real gum, preferably bubble gum, anything but sugarless — Alex seemed content to wait at the gate, flipping through a rock 'zine she'd brought from home.

They were twins, supposedly identical.

Twins and witches — T'Witches — no way around it, that's what they were.

Cam shrieked as a pair of hands fell heavily onto her shoulders. The stinging scent of aftershave filled the air.

"Whoa. Chill. It's just me." She was turned around gently to face Jason Weissman, grinning big, surprised, and stoked to see her. "You came to see me off," he marveled.

Jason's four-day weekend away with the guys! Did it start today? Cam looked around and saw Mike and Rick, Jase's buddies, on the check-in line a few gates over. She had totally forgotten. Instantly, she pulled down the sunglasses that had been perched on her head, holding back her long auburn hair, and tried to return Jason's smile — which normally was so not hard to do.

The star of the high school basketball team, he was a head taller than Cam, rippled and sinewy with broad shoulders, thick black hair, and dark brown eyes ringed with long black lashes that should have been illegal on boys. The only thing not dark about the seventeen-year-old high school senior was his personality. Jason was usually sunny-side-up boy. Which, today, was underscored by the bicep-baring, pec-stretched, yellow tennis shirt he was wearing.

He was also one of the few guys Cam couldn't completely fool. Her flirtatiousness only went so far with him. She really liked Jase. And he'd never tried to hide how much he cared about her. Their friendship had deepened over the past year. It was now, she liked to think, at the brink of the boyfriend-girlfriend thing. And she knew he wouldn't settle for half-truths or smiley-face small talk.

"You look shocked to see me, which translates into you forgot," he said now, reading her perfectly and shrugging. "Okay, that's cool. But what are you doing at the airport? What's the matter, Cam? You look like you're about to bolt or cry."

Apparently, her sunglasses weren't doing the trick. She stared at him through the dark lenses, trying to think of an answer — one that was decent without being damaging.

I'm going to an island to say good-bye to one of my oldest friends in the world, she could have said. *An ancient warlock who died saving my life — mine and*

Alex's — *from a pair of psycho brothers who happen to be our murderously deranged cousins.*

Or how about, *"Ooops, Jase, I forgot to tell you — and I hope it won't change our relationship — but Alex and I are witches."*

"Seriously, Cam, are you in danger again?" The rangy hottie knew she and Alex were magnets for trouble. He glanced quickly over his shoulder to signal his crew that he'd be right there. "You can trust me, Cami. What's up?"

Her sappy smile still in place, she came up with the totally lame, "Nothing," fixing her gaze on the miniature orange basketball charm he wore around his neck. She'd bought him that as a good-luck charm for the league championships.

"Then why are you acting so weirded-out to see me? I told you Rick, Mike, and I were splitting for the week-end —" Jason shoved his hands in his pockets, a sure sign he was getting uncomfortable.

"I'm not weirded-out, I was just . . . preoccupied." Cam attempted casual but came off strained.

"You stink at lying — even behind those dark shades. Come on, Barnes, I know you too well."

You really don't, she almost blurted aloud. *You know only one version of me. The other, the things you don't know and I can never explain? And if I tried? You probably wouldn't believe it, anyway.*

"Cami," Jason reached out to grasp her shoulder again. To his surprise, she flinched. "Wha —? Hey, I'm sorry. But you're freaking me now." He forced a grin, trying to lighten the mood. "Okay. You're not here to see me off. Where are you headed?"

Not daring to look at him, she mumbled, "You know, uh, the Midwest."

He nearly laughed for real. "That's a lot of territory. What state are you starting in?"

A state of emotional turmoil, she felt like saying. He was still staring at her, his intelligent mahogany eyes questioning, his smile down a notch. The vein on the left side of his forehead throbbed, a clue to how wigged he really was. She cleared her throat. "This trip came up at the last minute —" *Well, at least that was true.* Cam scanned the waiting area, as if she would find the end of her sentence somewhere in the crowd. "It's a family thing."

"Your mom and dad here, too?" Now Jason looked around.

"No, they're . . . uh . . . coming later. I mean . . . they might."

But they weren't. Not Dave and Emily Barnes, the parents Jason knew about.

Emily, Cam's adoptive mom, believed Cam and Alex were on a hastily scheduled class trip to Washington, DC, for the weekend. She assumed that her husband had signed the consent form.

David Barnes had driven the twins to the airport. He knew where they were going and why. He had known and been very fond of the old warlock Karsh. They'd met at a paranormal convention fifteen years ago — Karsh had quizzed him about his work, his wife, and their wish to have a child. The very next day, Dave had recently told his adopted daughter, Karsh delivered an infant girl to them, who they named Camryn.

No, Dave, who knew the truth, and Emily, who didn't, were not going to Coventry. But there'd be other family waiting there — the woman who'd given birth to them, the beloved old man who'd kept them safe. The first was waiting to see them, to get to know them; the other was waiting to be buried.

Alex Fielding had caught the tail end of the awkward encounter between Jason and Cam — the sister she'd met only a year ago and had, it felt like, lived a dozen lifetimes with since then.

Or maybe only one: Karsh's. He'd delivered the newborn Alex to Crow Creek, Montana, to Sara Fielding, a loving and trusted protector. After Sara died, the wise old warlock carried Alex clear across the country to Marble Bay, MA, to live with Cam, the twin she barely knew.

Alex's stomach twisted, as if she, not Cam, was standing outside the snack shop, put on the spot in her most vulnerable moment. She wished she could help, make up a story Jason would buy, and send it to Cam telepathically. She came up empty. Quick quips and caustic cover-ups were Alex's stock-in-trade. Now they were way out of reach. She was too raw; her skin ached, if that were possible.

She felt badly for Jason, too, so caring and crushed on Cam, yet so clueless right now. Alex wished she could tell him to back off.

She hadn't meant to eavesdrop on her twin and the would-be boyfriend. Shifting uncomfortably on a stiff waiting-area chair, she had been trying to lose herself in a magazine. It just hadn't worked. Her hand kept drifting to her necklace, the hammered half-moon dangling from a gold chain around her neck. And her thoughts kept drifting to Karsh, who'd given the necklace and so much more to her. And never would again.

Against her wishes, the awful scene in Salem Woods battered Alex's brain. She could still hear the sickening sounds of the hurled rock smashing against Karsh's head, of the beloved warlock falling hard to the ground. Rage at his killers boiled up in her once again. She could see them, her idiot cousins, Tsuris and Vey, lurching out of the forest. Smirking, seething with misguided rage, they'd come to harm Ileana, turned their wrath on the twins, and stayed to kill Karsh.

And the ancient warlock who'd loved and protected them always had known what would happen. He'd known that entering those woods was dangerous to him, that this time, helping Cam and Alex, as he had done all their lives, would mean sacrificing his own.

This Ileana had told them afterward, after Tsuris and Vey mindlessly hurled their stones, brought down the beloved old warlock, and set the wheels of fate in motion for this terrible trip.

Their flight was being called.

Alex opened her eyes, relieved to be distracted from the painful memories of that day. Her gaze drifted to Jason. He'd given them a lift to Salem Woods that fateful day. He'd seen them at home hours later, bruised and bloodied. No wonder he was worried about Cam now.

Jason was sweet and smart, an all-around good guy — if tall, athletic, Banana-garbed preppy was your type. (It wasn't Alex's.) He wore his President-of-the-Cam-Fan-Club status like some badge of honor. Now he was keeping his voice steady, but inside, b-ball boy was freaking out.

With her full-tilt witchy hearing and mind-reading skill, Alex was aware of Jason's heart thudding. He knew

Cam was holding back, nervous, afraid, suffering. He knew there was something she wanted to tell him but couldn't. He'd racked his brain trying to figure out what was going on — and had suddenly and stupidly decided that she might be breaking up with him.

Yo, it is so not about you, Alex wanted to holler. Her sister was a mess. Right now Cam's feelings for Jason were beyond beside-the-point. P.S.: There was *nothing* he could do to ease her pain.

Which didn't mean Jason would stop trying. Alex heard him say, "This is something big, isn't it? And it's something bad. I can see it in your eyes."

Cam's eyes. Right. Her extraordinary, future-seeing, flame-throwing, gorgeous gray eyes could see things that not even her talented identical twin could. But at the moment? The girl with the see-through sight was blind to the level of Jason's feelings for her.

Should I send her a telepathic message? Alex pondered. Would that make it better or worse?

Worse! Way worse, Cam immediately responded to Alex's silent question. *Any more input and I'll lose it. My head will explode!*

Now Cam, too, heard their flight being called. Boston to Green Bay. Boarding now.

True to her words, unspoken though they were,

Cam finally did lose it. In the middle of the airport, between gates 20 and 21A, she clutched her stomach and broke into wracking sobs, a full-out composure collapse.

Before Jason could react, Alex raced over and embraced her sister. "Hey, Jase-face," she said gently, knowing that he'd blame himself for making her cry. "She'll be okay. She's just dealing with some pretty heavy stuff."

The look on his face, a combination of dread and panic, was what made Alex add, "We both are. We're going to a funeral."

She had probably made Jason feel even worse, Alex thought, hurrying with Cam to the boarding line. But it had forced him to back off, kept him from asking more questions. And it had the added bonus of being true.

Before stepping into the plane's entry tunnel, Alex turned to give the confused boy a reassuring smile. But he was already gone. . . . Mike and Rick were looking perplexed. Alex followed their gaze and caught a glimpse of Jason, dashing out of the boarding area back toward the ticket counters.

CHAPTER TWO
COMING HOME

Green. Vibrant and clean, wonderfully fresh and alive. Her senses heightened, her heart sang. Here, she'd been born. Here, her family had lived. Here, she belonged. Alex Fielding and Coventry Island: love at first sight. It happened that fast.

Cam's reaction was lightning quick, too. And opposite.

Foreign. Remote and disconnected, thick with dark, tangled trees, ringed by a rocky beach, deserted but for a few seagulls and shells. Lots of shells. Camryn Barnes set foot on her birthplace feeling as out of place as she'd ever been anywhere.

Suddenly and unexpectedly, she was grateful she

and Alex had been wrenched from here, pulled apart, sent to grow up separately. This place, a haven for witches and warlocks, had not been safe for them back then. It felt the same way now. She wished she were anywhere but here.

Coventry was hard to get to. The island could only be accessed by ferry, but few from the mainland ever made the trip. It was nearly impossible to see beyond the forest or to expect there was anything of interest to see. Just one of dozens of small, heavily wooded islands off the coast of Wisconsin. It seemed uninhabitable.

Which was just the way the people of Coventry wanted it. Better if no one knew a complex, bustling community thrived there. Long-lived, learned, peaceful, and proudly self-sufficient, the island had been settled long before most of today's mainlanders were even born.

There was only one man, an old-timer named Burton "Bump" Rodgers, who knew how to get there and could be persuaded to ferry people to Coventry's shore.

"Witch Island?" Bump had laughed at Cam and Alex. "You girls sure that's where you want to go? No electricity, telephones, TVs. No cars allowed — guess they get around on broomsticks." His beady eyes narrowed. "It's told some folks never come back . . ."

Then he'd smirked at Alex, taking in her obviously

dyed, pink-tipped jet-black spikes and frayed denim jacket. " 'Course some folks belong there: witches, warlocks, and them. Which witch are you?" His big potbelly shook as he guffawed at his own pathetic joke.

"Careful," Alex had playfully warned him, narrowing her startling gray eyes at Bump. "We may have to cast a spell on you."

"We're just visiting." Cam elbowed her twin. That was the truth, wasn't it?

"Don't worry, Apolla, no one is going to force you to stay."

The voice calling Cam by her birth name jarred her. It seemed to float from the forest. Familiar but soft, it was completely absent of its normal snappishness.

"Ileana?" Cam called out timidly, "Is that you?"

"Who were you expecting, Glinda? Sabrina? The Wicked Witch of the West?" Again, the intended sarcasm fell flat.

Cam heaved a sigh of relief, hurrying toward the forest now. Ileana, at least, was safe and familiar.

The day of their birth, their father, Aron, had been slain; their grief-stricken mother, Miranda, had vanished. Ileana had been appointed guardian of the newborns though she herself was only a teenager. She'd done her best to keep the twins safe from those who would harm them, especially the powerful Lord Thantos DuBaer, their uncle who, until recently, was believed to be their father's killer.

Alex smiled at the sound of Ileana's voice. But her smile froze the minute she spotted her.

Cam gasped.

Was this a mirage? Were they seeing Ileana through a fun-house mirror? Impossible that this gaunt, disheveled woman was their fiery, haughty, staggeringly beautiful, and vain witch guardian. She, who wore only the up-trendiest designer labels, and jetted around the world on the arm of a famous movie star, was gone. In her place stood a frail replica, her eyes dull, her once lustrous hair brittle, uncared for.

Saddest and most shocking of all was the cloak hanging limply from her shoulders. Midnight-blue silk, it was soiled, stained. With what Alex wasn't sure, but Cam identified it immediately. Blood.

Ileana had worn it the day Karsh died. Had she not taken it off since?

She seems so . . . helpless, Alex telegraphed to Cam.

"Helpless, am I?" Normally, Ileana would have railed at the affront, cast a spell, turned them into some little groveling two-headed creature. Now all she could manage was, "If I'm so helpless, you won't be needing me. I'll show you where you're staying and be on my way."

"Sorry, we didn't mean it that way," Cam apologized.

"Don't insult me further by lying," Ileana replied wearily. "Just follow me." They trailed her into the woods. Alex hoisted a beat-up duffel over her shoulder and easily kept pace with their strangely sluggish guardian. Cam, whose suitcase-on-wheels bumped clumsily over rocks and jutting roots, hurried to keep up.

Not even the shock of seeing a bedraggled Ileana could keep Alex from breathing in the rich scents of the forest. She felt instantly energized, almost overpowered by its lushness. The sandy soil and pine needles gave way to brilliant foliage. Amid many shades of green were pink azaleas, white birches, cherry trees in early spring flower, purple and white lilacs, and golden forsythia. Alex was awed and amazed. Every single fragrance was familiar to her, remembered, a sensual memory long buried, now awakened. Comforting and consoling — this was hers.

What Alex took in, Cam, without meaning to, pushed away. She didn't stop or even pause to smell the roses — or anything at all. Seeing the one person who could make her feel safe, so changed, admittedly helpless, sent Cam zooming back into the panic zone. There, she babbled nonstop to hear the sound of her own voice, to make sure it was the same upbeat one she used in Marble Bay, where she was now sure she definitely belonged!

"Where are we going? Where are we staying? Is there, like, a hotel or something? Or maybe a Country Inn? I'm so totally up for a hot shower. I mean, there *is* running water, right?"

Ileana ignored her. Cam added, "Do cell phones work here?" She had a burning need to call home, to connect with her best bud Beth and her other friends who, like Jason, knew nothing about this part of her life.

Telepathically, Alex asked, *Did you bring a bathing suit?*

Cam scrunched her forehead. *What are you talking about?*

This isn't spring break, MTV-girl. Hotels? Cell phones? Your friends? What's next? Pop idol contests? Aloud, Alex said, "So we're probably staying with our . . . with Miranda? How is she?"

"No — and deluded," Ileana answered, not turning to look at them. "Your mother still trusts Thantos. She's with him at Crailmore."

"Crailmore?" Alex repeated. "What's that? Coventry's version of a mental institution?" At once, Alex wished she could take back that crack. Their long-lost mother, Miranda, had spent years locked away in a "clinic" in California.

Ileana stopped abruptly and whirled on them. A

spark of her old self returned. "How little you know. Crailmore is the DuBaer estate. It's been in the family for generations."

"Can we go there? Can we see her?" Cam asked nervously, unsure that she even wanted to.

"You're not prisoners here, go wherever you want. No doubt you'll receive an invitation to Crailmore. Thantos knows you're here."

"So this Crailmore place," Alex asked, "is that where our parents lived? Where we were born?"

"We were probably born in a hospital . . ." Cam started, and then regarded her woodsy surroundings, "or not."

Ileana sighed wearily. "There's a quota on questions. You've used yours up."

But a few minutes later, she relented — possibly just to silence Cam, who'd returned to babble-land. "Aron and Miranda got married and built their own home, LunaSoleil." *Loona So Lay,* she pronounced it. "Moon and sun. That's where you were born."

"So we'll be bunking there?" Alex asked, thrilled by the idea.

Until Ileana shot it down. "You've exceeded the question-quota. Besides, we're here."

An abrupt clearing in the wood revealed a stone

cottage. Ileana's house, they instantly understood, underwhelmed. There was nothing regal or pretentious about the modest stone cottage, nothing palatial, extravagant, or exceptional announcing, "A Goddess Lives Here."

Unless you counted the astonishing herb garden. Here, colorful, fragrant, and lush plants grew high, wide, and bountiful, looking every bit as wondrous as their magical properties.

Staring at it from the gate, Alex was awed. "This *rocks*. Does everyone on Coventry have these? Gardens to, you know, to help do stuff?"

"Do stuff?" Ileana shook her head. "Right, that's why we grow herbs. To do stuff."

Alex felt chastised. Cam came to her rescue. "I can recognize some of them. Lavender . . . rosemary. Those sprigs are . . . myrtle. And isn't this the one . . ." — she pointed to an aromatic plant with sparse leaves — ". . . the one Karsh called skullcap? It makes you sleepy, right? And there's mugwort, for the traveling spell."

A ray of pleasure pierced Ileana's cloud of doom. Karsh would be *so* proud of the twins. She couldn't wait to tell him —

Her face fell, remembering.

She snapped, "Flora-appreciation hour is up. Take the keys."

"Aren't you coming in with us?" Cam was instantly nervous.

Not now. Not tonight. I can't face this place, Alex caught Ileana thinking.

"Where will you go?" she asked.

"I'll spend the night at Karsh — that is, Lord Karsh's cottage. I've things to deal with there."

"Is that where . . . ?" Cam began.

"He is? Where his body is?" Alex finished her sentence.

Ileana flinched but raised her head regally. "Of course not. As befits an Exalted Elder, Lord Karsh lies in state at the Unity Dome, where tomorrow's ceremony will take place."

She seemed ready to say more but paused, bit her lip to keep it from trembling, then turned abruptly and left them.

Cam began to hyperventilate as an unwelcome flashback attacked her. Once, when she'd been about five years old, she'd gotten separated from her mom in a big department store. She'd only been lost for a little while, but the overwhelming panic of feeling abandoned had made her stomach lurch. Exactly as it was right now.

Sensing her sister's alarm, Alex quickly explained, "She's not abandoning us. Our guardian witch can't deal,

19

apparently, with her own home. Let's check into Casa Ileana and find out why."

Three slate steps led to the front door, which Alex bounded in one exuberant leap.

Cam lagged outside to take stock of her surroundings in case she got lost. Or something. Anyway, she was in no hurry to cross the threshold into Cousin Ileana's.

Alex let herself in. It took her eyes a minute to adjust. The slice of sun from the open front door was the only light in the dark, damp, and chilled room. Probably from being left empty for several days. She drew the curtains apart.

And stiffened, stunned.

Someone *had* been there. Someone who'd turned Casa Ileana into Casa Trash-eana. A demolition derby of wanton destruction confronted her. Ileana's sitting room had been ransacked, furniture viciously ripped apart, keepsakes, laptop, lanterns, photos, vases smashed, strewn across the floor. Even the skylights were broken. That accounted for the dampness and cold.

No wonder she couldn't face this place, Alex thought.

"Who would do this?" Cam came rushing up behind Alex. "Who hates her this much?"

The answer was a gimme.

Tsuris and Vey, the overgrown dolts who put the

"sin" in cousins. They blamed Ileana for their father, Fredo's, current jailbird status — it meant nothing to them that he was . . . hel-*lo!* . . . guilty! They were out for Ileana's blood, but apparently settled for wrecking her home.

Anger twisted in Alex's gut. If only she knew Coventry well enough, she'd rout out the spiteful, murdering slobs and show them what real revenge looked like.

They surveyed the destruction.

"You think?" Cam wavered, reading her sister's mind.

"Yeah, I do," Alex said. Ileana's damaged home was like a reminder of the proud witch's broken soul. What choice did she and Cam really have? They would roll up their sleeves and make it right, pick up the pieces of Ileana's . . . life.

While Alex used her telekinetic power to float Ileana's keepsakes, knickknacks, and clothing back to their original places, Cam picked her way through the rubble, cleaning up the old-fashioned way. A gold-framed picture drew her eye. Cam stared at it and smiled.

An astonishingly beautiful woman — so much more radiant than the woman they'd met only last week — her hair long and chestnut-colored, her eyes luminous and gray, stared back at her. The woman's arm was wrapped protectively around the shoulders of an exquisite blond-haired, beaming child. Miranda and Ileana.

Cam called Alex to come look. "She was something else back then, wasn't she? Miranda."

"A regular babe." Tears welled in Alex's eyes, though she wiped them away hastily. "That's what Karsh once said."

"I wish she'd come to meet us. Do you believe she's really at that Crailmore place?" Cam asked.

"Under the watchful and healing presence of dear Uncle Thantos?" Alex retorted sarcastically.

"Well, what are we waiting for? Let's find out." Cam flipped open her cell phone.

Alex snickered, "You're gonna *call* her? How? Oh, wait, I can just hear the conversation." She put on a computer voice. "'AT&T Direct. City and state, please.'" Alex then mimicked Cam, whining, "'Don't you have a listing for Coventry Island? No, there's no address. They don't *do* addresses there. Can't you just connect me with Crailmore?'"

Cam frowned. It irked her when Alex was right. "Well, maybe somewhere in this mess there's a phone book." She refused to give in.

Alex crossed her arms. "Yeah, I'm sure everything works exactly like in Marble Bay. Give it up, Camryn. If we want to contact our mother right now, our best bet is telepathy."

Cam sighed. "Right. And if Mom . . . Miranda was healthy and had her powers back, she'd have contacted us by now."

Unless she doesn't want to see us. Cam's thought, but Alex reluctantly agreed.

Cam needed to keep moving to keep that thought away. She went back to her search-and-rescue mission using her extraordinary eyesight to find and retrieve anything that might be valuable to Ileana. Underneath an especially dense pile of wreckage, she telescoped in on a painting. The canvas had been viciously slashed; still, you could tell it was a portrait of Karsh. The wise and loving warlock who'd been a grandfather to them: his smile kindly, his eyes twinkling — so alive! For some stupid reason, the portrait suddenly became too heavy for Cam and slipped out of her hands.

Alex picked it up. "It's not just that he's gone, is it?" Alex said intuitively. "You're freaked about the funeral."

Cam shook her head, denying it.

"Like Jason said, you stink at lying. Give it up, Barnes," Alex coaxed.

"I've never been to a funeral before." There, she'd said out loud what she'd refused to even silently admit to herself.

A surprising wave of tenderness washed over Alex. She knew just then how far she'd come. Or maybe it was being here on Coventry. But instead of her normal reaction, "Oh, poor, pampered, sheltered you," she heard herself comforting Cam. "It'll be all right. We'll be there together. Just squeeze my hand if you get scared. I'll protect you."

Alex broke Cam's melancholy mood. "Oh, you will? Who'll protect you? Let's see, due to death, devastation, and loss of powers, the usual suspects — Karsh, Ileana, and our long-lost mama, Miranda — seem to be unavailable."

Alex lifted her chin proudly. "I'm tough, I don't need protection."

There were noises outside the cottage, footsteps on the cobblestone path, and they both jumped!

Sensing danger, Cam focused her powerful eyes on the door. She'd stun whoever it was, blind the intruder. Alex telekinetically sent a broken chair leg into her extended arm. Holding it high, she so hoped it was Tsuris and Vey, just stupid enough to return to the scene of the grime-crime. This time, the T'Witches were ready.

CHAPTER THREE
A WALK IN THE WOODS

"You look shocked to see me," the visitor exclaimed, taking in Alex's defensive posture and Cam's electrically alert eyes.

Disappointed but relieved, Alex put her weapon down and telegraphed Cam, *That's the second time today someone's said that to you.*

"Really? Someone else surprised you first?" His half-smile, half-smirk threw Cam for a loop.

Shane . . . Shane Wright? Warlock, mind reader, ultimate fly-guy. Once, they'd despised and distrusted him. He'd come to them as Thantos's messenger, but during the course of his mission had done a lifesaving 180 and fought against their villainous uncle.

"How'd you know we were here?" Cam stammered, hoping he couldn't hear her heart thudding. She'd forgotten how magnetic the tanned, tawny boy was.

He grinned and ran his fingers through his wavy hair, grown longer and a lot lighter since she'd last seen him; streaked with blond, it now brushed his shoulders. "Everyone on the island knows who you are and that you're back."

We are, Alex agreed silently.

Not for good, Cam thought at the exact same moment.

Shane raised an eyebrow, amused. "Look-alikes don't think alike."

The twins frowned at each other. Then Alex turned her wary gaze on Shane. "So what are you, the warlock welcome wagon?" She was no fan of his and didn't really care if he knew it. Just because he'd refused to kill when Thantos ordered him to, didn't mean they could trust him.

"Busted," he conceded good-naturedly. "On what you said, *and* what you were thinking. I did come to welcome you, and I hope you'll both come to trust me."

"Sweet." Alex let the sarcasm drip. "Only, bad timing of epic proportions. Check it out." She motioned to the debris-strewn room. "A wreck-o-rama."

"Courtesy of Morons, Inc.," Cam added dryly. "Also known as our cousins, Tsuris and Vey."

"Fredo's sons did this?" Shane seemed to notice the mess for the first time. He frowned and shook his head sympathetically. I can help you clean it up, if you want," he offered.

"No. We should do this ourselves. Ileana's our cousin."

Cam couldn't hide her disappointment. Alex was dismissing him. He'd been here all of three minutes.

Alex softened. "Look, do your welcome thing for Cam. Let me deal with this."

"You sure?" Cam and Shane asked at the same time.

Hoping they didn't lock pinkies or do something equally cheesy, Alex dismissed them. "Go. Just be back soon."

With mixed emotions, Cam followed Shane outside.

Besides being buff beyond belief, the young warlock, who she'd first met in Marble Bay, was a bridge between her two worlds. Who better to help her *bond* a little with her . . . uh . . . native place? To feel whatever Alex was obviously feeling about Coventry. All she'd felt so far was the urge to leave. Then Shane walked in.

"I really did want to be the first to welcome you," Shane said as they headed into the woods that surrounded Ileana's cottage.

Cam tried but could not wipe the smile off her face or settle the flipping thing her stomach, acting independently, had decided to do. There'd been a magnetic attraction between them from the moment they'd met months ago in Marble Bay. She'd never been able to shake the feeling. The way he was staring at her now was so not helping.

An uninvited thought drifted by, and she tried to brush it away. Jason. Sweet, caring, and daring, the hometown boy she'd left behind would do anything for her. Had she ever felt this way around him?

Shane did the half-smile thing at her. Had he heard that thought? When she felt his arm rest lightly across her shoulders, it was, she told herself, a comforting, friendly embrace — nothing more. She didn't pull away, just savored being with him as they followed a path through the forest.

"Where are we going?" she asked. "Do you live near here?"

He shrugged and looked away. "I used to live about a mile and a half away. My family still does."

"You moved out?" she guessed.

"I got kicked out."

"Really?" What could Shane have done to get himself expelled from home?

"Difference of beliefs." He answered her unspoken question with jarring swiftness. "They brought me up to believe as they do and didn't like it so much when I began to question their, uh, loyalties." He tried to sound like it wasn't a big deal, but Cam suspected otherwise.

"Was it about Thantos?" she ventured.

"They're faithful to Lord Thantos. They think I'm not."

"Is that how things are divided here?" she blurted without thinking. "You're either with Thantos or against him? Can one person be that influential? I mean, he's not the president or anything."

Shane swung around to face her. "You have to understand, Cam. The DuBaer family is royalty here. For better or worse, they're powerful and influential. So, sure, people have strong feelings about them. But like anywhere else, there's the usual stuff that divides people: jealousy, greed, even love."

A strange feeling of uneasiness swept over Cam. "So where do you live now? Other side of the tracks or something?"

Had Shane squirmed or was she imagining it? "I'm bunking with a friend," he murmured, looking a lot like he wanted to change the subject.

He didn't have to. The subject changed itself.

There was no breeze, yet Cam shivered suddenly. The hairs on the back of her neck rose. This was not a premonition nor a vision. But her senses became razor-sharp. She felt like prey in the woods. She knew . . .

They were being watched.

She swiftly checked over her shoulder, but before she could focus through the screen of branches, leaves, and thick bushes, Shane asked, "What's wrong?"

Cam was embarrassed. It would seem so weird, so . . . babyish. *Someone's here. Someone's watching us.* "Uh, nothing." She quickly switched gears. "Tell me about the island."

The watchers waited in the woods. Waited for Apolla and Artemis, for Camryn and Alexandra. The twins had to be careful. Careful where they wandered and with whom.

Oh, really? And how would you know? Ileana asked herself cynically.

She'd witnessed it, but had been helpless, unable to save Karsh from death. Nor, for the first time, could she help her young charges that awful day in the Salem Woods.

But that wasn't why she'd been brought to her knees, devastated and debilitated.

Just before Karsh died, she'd gotten what she'd wished for all her life: to know who her real father was. Karsh had promised to tell her one day. Before he could, she'd found out. The one person on Earth she hated more than anyone, her sworn enemy, the vile Lord Thantos. He was her father.

That was the moment Ileana had lost it, ceased being herself.

To say the least.

She seemed to have lost the supernatural skills and hypersharp senses that had made her an outstanding witch.

So it was very likely that the feeling she had, that Cam — or Alex — was wandering into dangerous territory, was totally wrong. Meaningless. A fear fueled by guilt.

Ileana should have been the one showing the twins around Coventry. She was, after all, their guardian. She should have been introducing Cam and Alex to those who'd heard of but never met, them: to the Exalted Elders of the Unity Council, to Karsh's many friends and grateful fledglings, to the island's best and brightest youngsters . . .

Instead, she paced the slate floor of Karsh's cottage, tracing with the soles of her feet the grooves the old man's tread had worn into the stones. Her orange tabby cat, Boris, lay in the corner, watching her.

Ileana's once flawlessly shimmering hair was still a mass of knotted curls. She hadn't rinsed the rust-colored spots from the blue gown she'd worn for far too long. The blotches were bloodstains. Karsh's.

Her bare feet were rough and dusty. She had cleansed them in soothing herbal baths but had no desire to choose or don a pair of proper shoes. In addition to the loss of her ability to cast spells, transmutate, transport herself, and sense trouble, Ileana seemed to have forgotten how to take care of herself. She'd accomplished nothing since returning to the island with her guardian's body.

Back and forth before Karsh's desk she strode, staring at the book *Forgiveness or Vengeance.* Carefully, she avoided glancing at the tall chair behind the desk. She could imagine the disappointed look the old warlock would be giving her if he were still here, if he were sitting in that carved wooden monstrosity, his bony fingers folded in a tent before him.

He would have suggested in his commanding way that Ileana ought to have made time to show the twins around the island.

Ordinarily, she would have.

But nothing was ordinary anymore.

Karsh, who'd been the only parent she'd ever known, was dead.

The twins' mother, Miranda, had returned to Coventry after an absence of fourteen years.

And the sickening revelation about Thantos . . . she would not go to that place.

From the desktop, the grieving witch again lifted the book in which Karsh's journal was hidden. It took all her energy to carry it as far as his armchair, less than a foot away.

On his deathbed, Karsh had spoken of a curse. Ileana had begun to wonder whether it might have something to do with a mysterious sleeping sickness. Every time the pale witch picked up *Forgiveness or Vengeance,* her arms felt leaden. When she tried to read his words, her eyelids grew unbearably heavy. Though she fought to stay awake, sleep always won. Thus she'd examined only two paragraphs of the story Karsh had urged her with his dying breath to read:

Ileana, precious goddess, guardian of Apolla and Artemis, my future has been shown to me and time is short. Therefore, I write this in haste. But, be assured, I am driven by love and truth, not fear.

By now, of course, you know that Lord Thantos DuBaer is your father and that Aron and Miranda's twins are your cousins. You and they share the greatness and danger of being DuBaers. What you do not know is that you carry, as well, the blood of another noble line, the Antayus clan.

*　　*　　*

This was the passage that always confused and tired Ileana. How could she be an Antayus? Impossible.

She knew that Karsh — respected mentor, mighty tracker, renowned and beloved warlock — was of the Antayus clan. But as Karsh himself confirmed in his journal, Ileana's vile father was a DuBaer. Her mother's maiden name was Beatrice Hazlitt.

And Hazlitt, as everyone knew, was neither a noteworthy nor noble name. In fact, it was Beatrice's lack of fine lineage that had turned Thantos's mother, Leila, against her.

If her father was a proud DuBaer and her mother a lowly Hazlitt, how then could Ileana carry the blood of the mighty Antayus clan?

Ileana sank back into Karsh's worn leather armchair. His sweet peppermint-and-thyme scent still clung to it. She longed to read more of the journal, to fulfill Karsh's dying request. But again, her weary eyes began to shut.

"Help me, Karsh," Ileana whispered as her closed lids locked out the little daylight left in the room.

Help me, Karsh.

She had whispered, spoken, even shouted those words for as long as she could remember. It was a habit not easily broken. Not even by Karsh's death, it seemed.

Against the black screen of her closed eyelids, colors began to swirl. Red, orange, purple. A sunset sky. Seen through strange black stripes . . . thick poles of wrought iron blackened by age . . . the bars of a prison window! Ileana was wracked with a deep, deadly coldness, the bone-chilling damp of a musty jail cell. The sunset she saw through the high prison window, she suddenly understood, was the last she would ever see. Whoever she was, wherever she was, she was doomed. Her execution would take place at sunrise.

Ileana fought to awaken, but something held her back, held her down. She was shackled to the stone floor. Heavy chains cut into her ankles and wrists.

"Confess!" a shrill voice demanded. "Repent!" a merciless one ordered. "I accuse Abigail Antayus," a third called out. A girl's voice, this last one, a mere child. "She's the one who enchanted me!"

Ileana woke with a start. Drenched in perspiration, her heart palpitating wildly, she sat up abruptly in Karsh's chair and tried to shake the terrifying nightmare from her mind. Her hand had fallen asleep. It tingled with pins and needles. She tried to lift it from the open book on her lap. Looking down upon it, she saw in Karsh's precise, cramped handwriting the sentence: *It began in Salem in 1692 . . .*

CHAPTER FOUR
THE BEGINNING

Ileana, beloved child, here is the tale as it was passed down to me. This much is history:

The Salem madness erupted when two little girls, nine-year-old Elizabeth Parris and eleven-year-old Abigail Williams, began behaving oddly — screaming curses, having "fits" or seizures, and falling into "trances." The girls and their friends, who began displaying similar behavior, had been listening to scary tales told by the Parris's Indian-Caribbean slave, Tituba.

Elizabeth, Abigail, and their friends were examined by local physicians — among them the eminent doctor Jacob DuBaer — and it was decided that they were under the influence of the devil.

The children were then subjected to terrible pressure and disgusting concoctions meant to "help" them reveal the names of Satan's followers, the witches who were causing their suffering. The terrified little girls named Tituba and two other women, one ill-tempered and disliked in the community, the other a helpless and possibly deranged beggar woman.

Thus it began. Soon, other "witches" were revealed. They were imprisoned, tried, and with few exceptions, found guilty and executed. Many who were named as witches were women whose behavior or financial circumstances — in other words, their independence — marked them as different from what was expected of them in the 1600s.

Our great ancestor Abigail Antayus Stetson was such a one.

At least four things set Abigail apart from the other women of Salem. She was a brilliant physician, though only allowed to tend to women. Though married, she was known and called by her maiden name. Her husband, Samuel Stetson, a ship's captain, treated her as an equal in all respects. And Abigail had a handsome dowry, which Captain Stetson allowed her to keep and spend as she wished.

So she was educated, esteemed by her husband, and wealthy in her own right. All of which went against what was considered right and proper in the Salem colony. There were many who believed that Samuel was too easygoing with his young wife, that he was too charmed by her beauty and brilliance. They grumbled that young Abigail, with her healing herbs and potions, had cast a spell over the admired captain. Why else would he let her wander the town at all hours tending to the sick and needy rather than keeping her at home where she belonged to care for her own family?

One who led the complaining chorus was Dr. Jacob DuBaer. This black-bearded bachelor used leeches, bloodletting, and harsh tonics in his practice. And was outraged that so many of Salem's women — and too many of his male patients, as well — preferred Abigail Antayus's methods to his own. In 1690, Samuel Stetson was killed during a storm at sea. Married at 17, widowed at 25, Abigail was left with three small children to care for and a tidy fortune, which many a man wished to share. Among those eager to wed the "poor widow woman" was Jacob DuBaer. But Abigail refused him.

Like your own father, dear Ileana, your great ancestor Jacob was a jealous and unforgiving man. Two years later, in 1692, he took his revenge by naming Abigail as one of the witches of Salem.

He wasn't exactly wrong. Indeed, Abigail was a "witch." Her creed, like ours, was to embrace and nur-

ture all the creatures of Gaia, or Mother Earth. She prac-
ticed her healing in keeping with our purpose: so that
all things might grow to their most bountiful goodness.

Of course, you will recognize those words as one
of the principles inscribed upon the Dome . . .

Of course, Ileana thought, feeling unexplainably tired again, she had stared up at those words as a child sitting on Karsh's lap, snuggling against his black velvet vest. The memory overwhelmed her. A river of unshed tears mounted inside her head, making it too heavy to hold up.

As Ileana drifted off to sleep, Karsh's journal sliding gently from her lap, another young witch was hearing the saying for the first time.

"So that all things might grow to their most bountiful goodness," Cam repeated, savoring the words.

"You never heard that?" Shane guided her over a fern-filled bog in the woods. "It's one of the sayings carved into the Unity Dome."

The grip of his firm hand, the intensity of his twinkling eyes, the obvious delight he took in teaching her about the island were more confusing than comforting.

Several times, Jason's face, his loving, concerned expression, his distress at the airport, returned disturbingly to Cam's mind. It was a handsomer face than Shane's —

but no way had she ever felt *this way* around him. "The Unity Dome," she repeated, bringing herself back to the present. "I haven't been there yet," she told Shane. "We're going there for the . . . service."

"Karsh's funeral."

Cam nodded. "So Coventry was settled in the 1700s." She tried to get Shane back on track. He'd been telling her about the island.

"As a refuge from prejudice and bloodshed on the mainland," he explained. "The first to arrive were escapees from the witchcraft trials. And some people of mixed African and Caribbean blood, slaves or free citizens who brought with them Chango rituals and Voodoo spells. Lord Karsh's ancestors were among them.

"Later, from the frontier, white settlers with special gifts — healers, rainmakers, water dousers — and Native American shamans, or medicine men and women," he added tactfully, "and immigrant Chinese soothsayers. Lady Fan's family — she's one of the Elders you'll meet tomorrow. Her family arrived in the 1800s during the building of the intercontinental railway. They all found their way here. To freedom."

"You know a lot about this place." Cam was impressed.

"You will, too," he assured her, "by the time you're initiated."

If I'm initiated, Cam thought, then quickly changed the subject. "Is Crailmore near here?"

"Crailmore's to the north and west, about as far as you can get from here and still be on Coventry."

"My . . . Miranda's there," she told him.

"I know," he said gently.

"Shane." Cam stopped suddenly and touched his arm. "You would tell me if you thought she was in danger, right? If you thought Thantos was harming her?"

He looked at her strangely. "Of course. But you're her daughter. You'd sense if she was in danger."

Cam wanted to believe him.

Then she felt it again. The certainty that they were being followed. Or watched. She whirled around and zoomed her telescopic eyes as far through the heavily wooded area as she could. She was able to see a great distance, tunnel-visioning through the dense canopy of leaves.

Nothing.

"Stop," she instructed him. "Just stay still for a second. And tell me you don't sense someone watching."

He hesitated, then let out a long sigh. "Sorry. But, no."

"So I'm being . . . childish . . . paranoid?" Cam asked, though now she knew she wasn't.

Shane leaned against the knotty bark of an oak tree. He was clearly trying to decide whether to tell her something or not. After a moment, he smiled — a signal that he'd made up his mind not to—and slid down the rough trunk of the tree, motioning for her to sit with him.

Cam lost track of time as Shane chewed on a fallen pine needle and described how he'd grown up here among family, friends, teachers. He was a star, more gifted in the ways of the craft than his friends or relatives. His giftedness was noticed — and, he thought, rewarded — by one of the most powerful warlocks on the island, Lord Thantos DuBaer.

"He took me in and trained me," Shane confessed. "I spent years learning from him, under his guidance."

"You lived at Crailmore?" she ventured.

"No. But every afternoon I'd spend with Thantos's trainers in the caves beneath Crailmore."

"Caves?"

"Underground, miles of them." Shane made a sweeping motion with his arm. "Sacred and secret caves. It's said that spirits of the dead can be summoned from there, that the walls hold long-buried secrets."

"Hmmm," Cam mused. "If walls could talk —"

"On Coventry, sometimes they can," Shane teased, flashing one of his disturbingly handsome, dimpled smiles at her.

"There's a maze of interconnecting underground tunnels on the island," he continued. "At one time, it was an underground railroad, a safe harbor for witches and warlocks who feared they were being hunted."

Ping! She felt it again. The word "hunted" tripped her inner alarm. She could practically feel eyes boring into her back. Someone, or some*thing*, was watching.

Shane stood abruptly. "We'd better get you back. We promised your sister."

They took a different path back, this one narrow, rocky, and dense with thick, jutting roots of ancient trees. Still, it was odd that Camryn-the-Coordinated should fall. One foot unexpectedly got caught under a half-buried plank of wood. She lost her balance and did an embarrassing face-plant into the dirt.

She wasn't hurt. But that wasn't the reason she refused Shane's outstretched hand.

Wood was not a conductor of electricity, yet Cam had felt a slight shock, an electric tingle shoot up her leg as she'd tripped. It grew stronger now as she pulled the board out of the earth and examined it carefully.

"Are you going to set it on fire?" Shane teased. "Punish it for tripping you?"

Cam ignored his attempt at cute.

Covered with a decade's worth of mold and dirt, the old plank could have been any random piece of wood in the forest.

Cam knew it wasn't.

She squinted. Even with her extraordinary eyesight, she could barely make it out, but something — a sign, a symbol — had been carved into the wood. "Do you see this?" She stood up and handed it to Shane.

He turned it over a few times and shook his head. "See what?"

Using her fingernails, Cam tore away more layers of impacted dirt. The board was very faded, washed by years of moisture. Still, she could tell. Once, someone had lovingly carved a design into this worn plank. Once, it had been a sign, perhaps hung over the doorway of someone's home.

Instinctively, her fingers felt for the necklace she always wore, a delicate gold chain bearing a sun charm. It fit precisely into Alex's moon charm, forming a perfect circle. The linked images, sun and moon, were the same design she could see in the plank she'd tripped over. There were words carved under the design. *LunaSoleil,* French for moon and sun.

"My parents' house is around here, isn't it? Can you . . . can we see it?" Trembling, Cam looked up into Shane's now-shaded eyes.

He turned away from her. "It was torn down years ago."

He was lying.

CHAPTER FIVE
A SAD GOOD-BYE

This much Ileana would do. She would take the twins to the Unity Dome to say a final farewell to the old warlock they all had loved.

For this she had bathed scrupulously. She had perfumed her scrubbed skin with rose water. Shampooed her hair with an infusion of flaxseed oil, aloe, and rosemary, then unknotted her tangled white-gold tresses with the wide-toothed comb Karsh had carved for her. Long ago. When Ileana was a child, younger than Alex and Camryn were now.

When she called the twins from the gate of her cottage, she could see in their eyes the wonder and approval she hadn't allowed herself to feel.

"Ileanna," Cam whispered, awed. "You look . . . beautiful."

"Like a goddess," Alex blurted.

Ileana's jaw tightened as she fought back emotion. "Not half as good as Lord Karsh deserves." She'd tried to sound crisp, matter-of-fact, but it had come out a weepy whisper. To pull herself together, she studied the twins severely. Cam was wearing a long, delicate dress that seemed familiar to Ileana, a gossamer gown of palest pink with slender shoulder straps.

"It's yours," Cam confessed, hoping her guardian witch would be okay with her choice. She really had no clue what was considered proper for a Coventry funeral. Everything she'd brought seemed beyond wrong.

And she could hardly look to Alex as an example.

Her born-to-offend sister was all about stark black. Tight black jeans, black work boots, and a black Spandex T-shirt. The only touch of color in Alex's ensemble was the faded patchwork quilt she had tossed across her shoulders like a shawl and the pink spikes in her hair.

Ileana didn't rage or rag on either of them. Sounding more like gentle Karsh than her perfectionist self, she merely sighed and said, "Oh, well, I suppose it's what's inside that counts."

They started through the woods. Above the tree

line, Cam and Alex caught sight of strange fireworks flashing.

"It's just sunlight bouncing off the glass panels of the Unity Dome," Ileana informed them. "Close your mouths. The bees have more important places to explore. And, if it makes you feel any better," she told them, "I, too, have never been to the funeral of someone who meant . . . so much to me . . . as Lord Karsh." He'd been both mother and father to her.

"I have," Alex murmured, thinking back again to the day her adoptive mother, Sara, had been buried.

That day, less than a year ago, griefstricken and alone, Alex had felt nothing but a deadly weariness. She hadn't been able to cry. Or feel. Or think. She'd been in Crow Creek, Montana, with no idea how or where she'd live. Then the cheerful sprite who she'd called Doc had shown up.

Pasty-faced with what Alex now knew was the white herbal cream he used to preserve his ancient skin, Karsh had returned her half-moon charm and told her he knew just the place for her. Before nightfall, she was two thousand miles from Montana, on Camryn Barnes's doorstep in Marble Bay, Massachusetts.

"Doc," Alex whispered aloud, as if he could rescue her now as magically as he had then. "Karsh."

"Will we have to see him?" Cam asked in a shaky voice. "I hope not. I don't think I can —"

"He will be there," Ileana said. "And those who wish to, will look upon the great tracker; those who prefer not to, won't. You can decide once we're in the hall. Have you thought yet of what you will say?"

Cam stopped abruptly. "Say?"

"About what?" Alex asked, although Ileana's thoughts made it plain that they were expected to offer a eulogy, to speak of what Karsh had meant to them.

"Many of his devoted fledglings will be participating —"

"Oh, no." Cam gasped. "I mean, he was *your* guardian —"

"I submitted your names to speak in my place. It's a great honor," Ileana assured them.

"We wouldn't think of depriving you of it," Alex shot back.

"Ungrateful fledglings!" the blond witch railed — sounding, Alex was glad to hear, like her irritable old self again. "Is my devastation not complete? After losing Lord Karsh, my dearest friend in the world, and now that grief has driven me nearly as mad and helpless as Miranda —"

"That's our mother you're talking about," Alex felt compelled to remind her.

Ileana ignored the interruption. "You want to make

my misery and humiliation complete? I will not stand, weak and defeated, before all who have known and envied me since I was a child!"

"Oh? And what, it's easier for us to face a mob of strangers and make fools of ourselves?" Cam asked.

"Exactly!" Ileana was relieved that they understood. "Far easier —"

"For *you*," Cam groused.

"Get over yourselves," Ileana commanded. "What difference will it make to you? No one here really knows you —"

Shane, Cam thought.

They were emerging from the woods, trekking toward the south gate into the village. "Shane?" Ileana had read that thought, loud and clear. "You care more about what one of Thantos's ex-lackeys thinks than about saving your guardian from disgrace," she accused.

"She said, 'shame,'" Alex quickly intervened, staring dumbfounded at the eruption of color around them. The buildings of Coventry Village were of every vivid hue. Small shops and houses, none more than three stories tall — except, still in the distance, the soaring Unity Dome — were painted purple and green, orange and turquoise, and decorated with rainbow pentagons, brightly striped awnings, and painted flower boxes overflowing with unseasonable blooms. There were café tables surrounding a pleasant village square, which was usually bustling. This morning, however, only waiters lounged there — and even they, Alex discovered by reading Ileana's mind, would leave their posts shortly to attend Karsh's funeral.

Soon they were caught up in the crowd flowing toward the Dome. Trembling at what she would see and say there, Cam took Alex's hand. Instantly, she felt again, as she had in the woods, watchers . . . eyes focused on her, heating her back, neck, and face.

What's going on? Alex asked silently as a racket of girls' voices assaulted her ears and Cam's hand grew hot and sticky in her own. *There they are. Not Spike-haired Blackie, the other one, Pasty-in-Pink. But, Sers, they look so . . . ordinary!*

I don't know, Cam answered. *It happened before. When I was with Shane.*

"Save your gossipy little secrets," Ileana said, hurt and anger mingled in her voice. "Try to remember why we're here." She stepped behind them and, with an arm on each of their shoulders, shepherded them swiftly through the slow-moving throng.

The big amphitheater already seemed full. Sunlight streamed through the dome down onto a plain pine coffin at the center of the arena. Three people bathed in light sat behind the raised casket.

"The little one is Lady Fan," Ileana whispered to them. "She's one hundred and two, if she's a day. The dotty old codger blowing his nose is Lord Grivveniss."

As she looked at the large, strangely beautiful brown woman in the center chair, Cam's eyes stung with tears.

"And that's Lady Rhianna," Ileana said, suddenly misty-eyed herself, "one of Karsh's oldest friends."

The regal woman's face was placid, but Alex could hear her inner grief, and the sorrow and love in Rhianna's silent sobbing shook Alex to her core.

Look, they're crying. She heard the sarcastic girl's voice again. *They are sooo mainland.*

People were filing past Karsh's coffin. Some of them paused silently, some merely looked, then moved on, and some laid flowers, herbs, crystals, or amulets in the pine box.

Ileana started down the aisle to the center of the arena. "No," Cam whispered, "I . . . I can't do it."

"I'm going," Alex said, following Ileana. Cam hesitated, looked over her shoulder at the seated, stricken strangers, then quickly scampered after her sister.

Ileana waited for them at the bottom of the stairs. With an arm around each, she led them behind the casket to introduce them to the three Exalted Elders. Lady Fan and Lord Grivveniss merely nodded. But Lady Rhianna rose as they approached.

"Apolla." She took Cam's hand, then Alex's. "And Artemis. I've waited so long to meet you." They felt the electric charge of her grip. It reminded Alex of the tingling sensation she'd gotten the first time she'd brushed against Karsh, when she'd mistaken him for a doctor at the hospital where Sara lay dying.

Holding onto their hands, studying their eyes, boring into their thoughts, the wild-haired witch smiled sadly. "As always, Lord Karsh was right."

Right? Cam tried to say aloud, but her mouth had gone dry and the word stuck in her throat.

"Right about what?" Alex asked.

But Lady Rhianna had turned to Ileana. "You have done well, reckless child. They will yet lead a dynasty."

As Rhianna embraced their guardian, Alex looked away and found herself staring at Karsh.

The sight drew a gasp from her, which was followed by all the tears she hadn't been able to shed for Sara. Awash in sorrow, hiccupping back sobs, Alex shut her eyes and pressed a fist to her mouth, trying to hold back the wild flood of emotion.

Her eyes flew open at the unexpected feel of something brushing her cheek. But it was a gentle caress. Soft as a first kiss, light as a summer breeze, it filled her with golden warmth. She turned to see who had touched her. Cam was still staring at Rhianna; Ileana gazed skyward at the great glass dome, her face bathed in streaming sunlight. If not them, who had tried to comfort her?

And then she knew. The one who had always reassured her . . .

Ashamed of her outburst, Alex blinked away her tears and looked, really looked at the adored old warlock in the plain pine coffin. "Cam, it's all right," she whispered. Karsh's face, warm brown and unlined as a boy's, was smiling contentedly beneath the worn halo of his nappy white hair. There was no scar left from the rocks that had cut him down, the rocks their terrible cousins, Tsuris and Vey, had thrown.

"No," Cam whispered. "I can't. I'll —" Her shoulder tingled suddenly, hummed with a strangely soothing vibration. She glanced up at Rhianna, who murmured to her softly, "You can, child. You must." Then, nodding with compassion, the majestic witch turned Cam gently toward Karsh's casket.

Like Alex, Cam was taken aback by how peaceful the beloved tracker looked, and by the smile suffused with love that seemed directed at her. His golden shroud glittered beneath a bounty of mourners' gifts. Before she knew what she was doing — and oblivious to the fact that Alex had the same thought — Cam began to unhook her sun charm as her sister unlatched her hammered-gold moon.

A cry from the front row of the amphitheater stopped them. They looked up into Miranda's alarmed gray eyes.

Cam blushed. Alex reddened, too, but her heightened color came from anger, not embarrassment or guilt. The mother they barely knew was sitting beside their uncle and old enemy, Thantos. And she hadn't even gotten up to come to them, to hug them. What spell had Thantos cast on her, or did she simply care more about him than her own children?

"Hold onto your amulets," Ileana advised them both. "You have no idea how Karsh schemed to make sure you won and wore them."

"But what can we give him?" Cam asked.

"Your heart in words," Ileana said.

Seven speakers, including Lady Rhianna, the most eloquent of all, had given their eulogies when Ileana signaled the twins that it was their turn.

"It's okay," Alex said, feeling Cam's hand begin to tremble again in hers. "I'll go first."

She had no idea what she would say. But as she walked past Karsh's casket and glanced at his still comforting face, she found herself silently asking him to speak through her . . . to help her find words, the right words that would please him. It was a crazy thought, she knew, and yet she could almost hear him — imagine him, anyway — saying yes.

A murmur started through the assembly as she mounted the podium and cleared her throat.

"Aron's daughter," she heard. "Which one?" "The impetuous one whose wildness Karsh loved." "Artemis, the moon child."

Alex laughed. Which quickly silenced the crowd. "I guess I don't have to tell you who I am," she said. "But I want to tell you that I myself didn't know . . . until Karsh — Lord Karsh — in all his black-velvet splendor . . . in clothing way cooler than my grotty tribute . . ." She plucked at her T-shirt, explaining her costume. "His face smeared in that 'white fright' concoction he wore . . ."

There were appreciative chuckles from the audience. And one caustic snort, which Alex traced to a trio of girls about her age, midway up the amphitheater, girls she'd never seen before. There was a vacant seat among them, which she only noticed because it was probably the only one left in the arena.

Clearing her throat, she continued. "Until he . . . until Karsh came to me in dreams. Gently and gradually, he let me know that I was not the geek, mutant, weirdo the kids at school called me — but someone . . . something . . . special. That what I had been frightened by and ashamed of were really magical gifts. Gifts to be re-

55

spected and cherished, because they were capable of helping me do great good. Karsh revealed to me that I was . . . one of you. A witch. And that a girl I'd seen with a frightening likeness to me was actually my sister, my long-lost twin."

She smiled at Cam then, seated between Lady Rhianna and Ileana, her eyes on Alex, glowing with pride. *You go, girl*, Cam telegraphed. Some of the spectators burst into laughter — those who were mind readers intercepted the message.

Alex laughed, too. "You have no idea how good it feels, how freeing to be among you, to not have to hide who and what I am, to know that though most of us have never met before, we know all about one another . . . I mean, I definitely get the feeling that you know all about me —"

"Bet on it, T'Witch girl," she heard. She turned toward the trio of young witches again. This time, the empty seat was filled. By Shane. Alex was about to nod at him when the girl to his right, a striking young witch whose glaring face was framed with long, wild, dark curls, suddenly wrapped her arms possessively around him and slithered her cheek against his.

Shane had a girlfriend! Alex stole a quick glance at Cam, who clearly hadn't heard or seen what Alex had.

"Um, you know me . . . because you're just like

me," Alex finished her thought. "That also is a gift Karsh has given me, given us . . . I miss him, and yet I know that he is still with us. He's with me, for sure," she said, unconsciously stroking the cheek that the ghost hand had caressed. "I feel his presence. I hear and see him fifty times a day. . . . I ask his advice and, guess what, I receive it."

Her remark was greeted with nodding heads, chuckles of recognition, and murmured agreement. "Yes." "It's true." "I feel the same way."

She was finished. She had said what she'd wanted to — or maybe what Karsh had wanted her to say. Alex felt complete. Connected. Home.

Karsh's death, though it left an aching emptiness in her heart, had been the bridge between her worlds.

Head bowed, she stepped down and moved toward her seat.

And Cam stood shakily.

She did not glance again at the casket. She walked past it, chin up. Trying furiously not to give in to the building tears, she stepped up to the podium.

"Karsh saved my life. I had everything, I thought — and some weird disease," she began. "I lived in the home Lord Karsh entrusted me to . . . a wonderful home with caring, loving people . . . parents, friends . . . Materially, I had everything —"

And I am a material girl, Alex heard one of the girls with Shane whisper.

"But . . . like Alex . . . um, Artemis, my sister, I thought something was . . . wrong. I tried to tell people about it. My mom —." Cam reddened furiously and could not look at Miranda, who sat at Thantos's side, facing her.

The burly tracker smiled at Cam's slip. It was hard to tell whether his expression was meant to pity, encourage, or ridicule her.

"Um, I mean, Emily, one of my protectors. I tried to tell her and my . . . Dave . . . and my best friends. . . . But all the while, the only one who really knew, knew and understood was —"

Alex expected to hear her name. Instead, Cam said, "Karsh. He always understood me. He brought me and my sister together. And he helped us every step of the way. I mean, really helped. As I said, he saved my life . . . more than once. I am sorry . . ."

The dam holding back Cam's tears burst at last. "So sorry that I couldn't save his," she sobbed.

Lady Rhianna hurried to the podium and reached to help her down.

As Cam was about to take a step she saw a face in the crowd. A face so out of place she thought she might be dreaming.

What was Jason Weissman doing here?

CHAPTER SIX
THE FURIES

Cam *had* to get to Jason. If it was Jason. The face she'd seen had worn a mask of shock, but the clear olive complexion, the dark eyes, midnight-black hair . . . A dream? If only.

Jason was here. In this, her other life.

How had he found her? What had he heard? And where was he now, Cam wondered desperately as Karsh's funeral service wound down.

As soon as she could, and without a word to Alex, Cam took off in the direction she'd seen Jason's face. Ileana's delicate dress kept tangling in her legs, slowing her down as her mind raced frenetically.

Where could he have gone? Toward the woods? The

lake? Into the village? He'd be alone, probably lost and bewildered. She had a wild, irrational thought. Maybe he was hungry.

Score on that last idea. Cam found Jason sitting at a deserted outdoor café in the village square. Elbows on the table, head in his hands, he looked like a confused stranger in a very strange land.

Her heart in her throat, Cam sped toward him but abruptly stopped several feet away. He looked up, and their eyes locked. At first, neither spoke. Then they talked at the same time, loosing a string of questions: What are you doing here? How'd you get here? What were you doing? What kind of trouble are you in? Did someone make you come here? What did you see?

Jason raised his palm. "Whoa. Okay, you go."

Biting her lip, Cam walked over to the table and forced herself to sit down. Urgently, she asked, "Please, Jase, I need to know. What are you doing here?"

"I came after you."

"Hello, obvious. But why?" Cam could hear the rising edge of hysteria in her voice.

He shrugged, trying to hide his embarrassment. "It looked like you were in trouble, like you wanted help but couldn't ask. I thought I . . ." he mumbled, "should be there for you."

He'd acted, he told her, out of fear, concern, and

though he didn't say it, she knew, love. She'd been an emotional wreck at the airport. Jason could not just walk away. He cared too much.

Cam thought she was out of tears. So wrong. The floodgates holding back her tears were about to burst as her heart ached for him, for his kindness. But all she could say was, "What . . . how much did you . . . see?"

"I don't know what I saw," he answered candidly. "Maybe you can tell me."

He'd found out where she and Alex were headed and changed his ticket. Once he landed in Green Bay, he'd asked around — Had anyone seen them? They were hardly inconspicuous. Identical but opposite. It had taken him a day and a half, but eventually he ran into an old ferryman who offered him a ride to Witch Island, where he'd taken the girls — a place from which, he'd hinted, Jason might never return. "What a crock, huh?" Jason laughed nervously.

"Totally." Cam pasted a wan smile on her face.

"Anyway," he continued, "I followed the crowd to that auditorium or whatever it was."

Cam exhaled finally, when Jason told her he'd arrived only to hear the very end of her eulogy and none of what Alex had said.

"You must have been close to the old guy who died," Jason probed, "this Lord Karsh."

She paused. "He was . . . like a grandfather —"

Jason's eyebrows arched. Why weren't Cam's parents there?

"— to Alex," Cam finished. A half-truth was better than a whole lie, she told herself.

"Oh." Luckily, Jason acted like that explained . . . some of it.

"He sort of brought us together," Cam continued carefully, hoping Jason wouldn't demand details. He didn't, but his next question tripped her.

"Was he royalty . . . or in some kind of club or cult? What was that lord stuff about?"

"Oh, no, it's not a cult," she rushed to assure him.

"This place is really weird." He laughed nervously again. "I feel like I just slid into another dimension."

Cam had never considered how to describe the people of Coventry to, well, her real-life family and friends. She'd never had to.

Today, her luck had run out. Now she had to deal. Jason needed an explanation that would satisfy him, prove to him that she wasn't in danger. In other words, she needed to tell a lie convincingly. Anything to get him to leave. Now would be a good time.

"Well, at least the ferry guy was wrong." He leaned back, tipping his chair. "There's no such thing as witches, so that can't be it. I mean," he tried to joke, "there's not a pointed black hat or cauldron in sight!"

Cam swallowed and hoped he didn't notice. "It's a kind of a special . . . community," she offered. "The people here — they're great — they're just different. Different in a good way," she clarified. "They're dedicated to helping others, to doing good things with their lives."

Jason looked doubtful. "Is it a commune? Like a hippie flashback?"

Excellent comparison! "That's a really good way to think of it," she said.

"Then what's up with all the secrecy?"

Oops, another question Cam was not prepared for.

"Jase?" Cam leaned in toward him and, because she didn't want to make eye contact, reached for the orange basketball charm that hung around his neck. "Sometimes, people are scared of what they don't understand. And it can get weird, you know?"

"I guess." He didn't seem to follow.

"So this part of our — I mean, Alex's life, she wants to keep it on the down-low. People already think she's weird! Imagine if all this got out." Cam felt like a traitor for that but pushed on. "You're . . . amazing. I mean, for coming here. I . . . don't know what to say. But anyway, I'm fine. Alex is fine. Not in any danger. No cause for concern. Basically."

He wasn't buying it. It was written all over his face. "You can probably still catch your friends in Florida," she said hopefully.

His jaw tight, he stared at her. "You want me to disappear," he said finally. "What are you hiding? Another guy?"

Cam was startled. Where had *that* come from? Jealousy was so not one of their issues.

"I'm sorry," he said. "Look, it's obvious you came here for a funeral. It's hard, I can see that, and why you were crying at the airport. But I keep feeling there's more. I can't shake the idea that you're in trouble. Maybe you don't want my help, but why are you pushing me away?"

"I need to do this Alex-family thing," she finally said. "I appreciate that you came after me, but honestly? There's nothing you can do here. You should just catch up with your friends and party like you planned. We can deal with all this bizarre stuff when we get back."

"Cam?" He put his hands on her shoulders as he got up to leave. "I can't believe I'm saying this. But I don't know if there'll be a 'we' by that time. If you can't be open with me, maybe there never was."

Cam's heart was breaking when, at the pier, she hugged him tightly. The ferry was approaching. She felt Jason's lips brush the top of her head. Had she been able to look into his soulful eyes and kiss him, she might have wiped away some of his doubts. But somehow she couldn't. She'd been shocked to see him and touched, but not grateful. She'd tried to make him understand . . . but she'd deceived him.

She couldn't tell him the truth. For lots of reasons. Surely, Shane wasn't one of them.

If Alex, the twin with the sharply honed hearing, was being followed instead of Cam, she might have deciphered the whispers of the watchers just then. She'd already caught their catty cracks at the funeral.

Cam, though, had neither glimpsed nor heard them. She'd felt their presence during her walk with Shane. Now, wrapped up in her unexpected little drama, Cam hadn't even sensed them.

Too bad for her. Too, too tasty for them.

They called themselves The Furies. Sersee was their natural leader, Epie and Michaelina, her faithful followers.

Had Cam and Alex grown up on Coventry, they'd have known these girls. They'd have known what they were up against and why.

Sometimes, ignorance is bliss. At other times, it's a death sentence.

"Life is just full of unexpected surprises," Sersee said gleefully to Epie and Michaelina. "I didn't think the saga of the princess power twins could get any more interesting. But apparently, it has. How touching was that little reunion?" Sersee cocked her head. She smiled in delight.

The violet-eyed witch wasn't the smartest or most talented teen on Coventry. She'd been passed over when Karsh had chosen his fledglings and hadn't impressed talent-scouting Thantos as Shane had.

Sersee had not forgotten either of those slights.

What she lacked in intellect she made up for in cunning. She was wily and played to her strengths: most notably, her ferocious beauty. Her dense tangle of jet-black curls fell nearly to her waist; her pale purple eyes were framed by long black eyelashes and dramatically arching eyebrows. Her porcelain skin was flawless, but little about her was soft. Beyond slim, she seemed all sharp jutting angles, all elbows, shoulder blades, cheekbones. Strikingly tall and thin, demanding, and issue-ridden, she'd have totally been an anorexic model on the mainland. On Coventry, she had higher goals.

Territorial, two-faced, and tricky, many of her performances were worthy of Academy Awards. Shane was her boyfriend, her property. She'd needed him, and she'd gotten him. In his eyes, her role was the wickedly fun-loving, good-hearted beauty. And she'd made herself totally available to him.

Those who crossed her found her playing a very different role.

And the Shane-struck twin, whether she knew it or not, had crossed her.

As far as Sersee was concerned, the minute Camryn had taken that walk with Shane she'd doomed herself.

Witnessing the tender good-bye scene between Cam and her homeboy was like a delectable dessert with an even sweeter surprise inside: a weapon Sersee needed. "Go now — on the ferry," she instructed Epie, the duller of her lapdogs. "Let's be sure . . . the Marble Bay boy . . . Jason . . . doesn't get far."

"What do you mean?" Epie was clueless.

"What do you think?" Sersee mimicked. "Prevent him from leaving Coventry."

Sersee's sarcasm flew over Epie's head. "Why?" she asked.

"Why? Why are you so thick!?" Sersee demanded. Epie wasn't following her logic, so she explained, "Insurance. Think of Cam's boy-toy as an insurance policy."

"For what?" The still blank Epie wanted to know.

Sersee's violet eyes flashed menacingly. "To make sure the new little darlings of Coventry don't overstay their welcome."

CHAPTER SEVEN
SECRETS AND CURSES

On the windswept side of Coventry, surrounded by iron gates and impressive statues, generations of DuBaers and other important families were laid to rest.

Some miles to the south, in a less grand graveyard, Karsh had been buried among his ancestors and, although it was known as the Antayus Cemetery, alongside witches and warlocks from dozens of different clans. Here, simple plaques laid flat in the grassy earth marked the graves of both the great and the anonymous dead. And here Ileana came on the afternoon of Karsh's burial.

The mourners were gone. The living had left. Clutching the warlock's precious journal, the young witch rested with her back against a tree between the fresh, flower-decked mound of earth warming Karsh's old bones and the bronze plaque that marked her mother's grave.

Beatrice Hazlitt DuBaer. The only DuBaer in the Antayus Cemetery, thanks to Leila DuBaer, Ileana's strong-willed grandmother. The arrogant old witch had undoubtedly insisted that Beatrice, her son Thantos's low-born wife, be banned from the DuBaer family plot.

On her mother's marker, Ileana had laid a sprig of lilac from her garden. She had gone back to Karsh's cottage after the graveside ceremony and found that she could no more be alone than she could stand to be among people who wanted to talk to, console, or pity her. So she had taken the book with her and come to the graveyard to be among the dead.

And to read about them.

She opened to the page where she had left off. The saga of Jacob DuBaer and Abigail Antayus continued.

In order to bring charges against Abigail, Karsh had written, *Jacob convinced several of his patients that their "rebellious" children were bewitched. He chose patients whose daughters were under the care of Abigail Antayus. It wasn't hard to draw a connection between Abigail's ministering and the "devilish" behavior*

of the little girls. But it proved difficult to get the children to testify against the beloved young doctor.

Difficult for an ordinary man, but Jacob DuBaer was no more ordinary than Abigail. Like her, he was a witch, a warlock afraid of being discovered. All his days as a doctor Jacob had turned his back on the craft, believing that he owed nothing to Earth or its creatures. But now, fear and vengeance drove him back to the old ways. So when threats and foul-tasting tonics failed, Jacob relied on magick. And succeeded. Two young girls swore that Abigail Antayus had enchanted them.

The good young physician was arrested.

But, as happened in rare cases, instead of other accusers coming forward, the court was flooded with angry citizens testifying to Abigail's charity and good character. After holding the widow in prison for one week, the judges were forced to declare her innocent and release her. They did so with a stern warning and, at the suggestion of her chief accuser, forbade her to practice doctoring in Salem from that day forth.

A punishment Abigail could not abide.

She and her young children left Salem for Marbletown, a village some miles away, which, in the late 1800s, was renamed Marble Bay. In Marbletown, Abigail continued to aid the poor and needy, training her daughters and son to do likewise.

Jacob DuBaer pursued her. Shamelessly, he urged her to unite their powerful families through marriage. When Abigail refused him a second time, he brought his charges of witchcraft to the court in Marbletown.

Here, Abigail had no relatives or friends of long-standing, no patients of any influence in the community. And here, Abigail was tried, found guilty, and, at the tender age of twenty-seven, hanged from the oak tree in what was then known as Witches Hill and is known today as Mariner's Park.

Mariner's Park in Marble Bay. Ileana knew it well. And knew that Karsh's legendary ancestor had died there. It was one of the Sacred Sites. It was also where the wise old tracker had given Camryn — the infant Apolla — to David Barnes, a protector.

As a young teen, Camryn had begun going to that exact spot in Mariner's Park. She'd never been told of its history — her history — yet somehow she'd sensed its power and had made it her retreat.

All that Ileana knew. Now Karsh was telling her that she, too, was related to the famous young doctor? How was that possible? It was her ancestor the treacherous Jacob DuBaer who'd had Abigail Antayus put to death. What branch of that family tree had produced Ileana?

As if to ask him, Ileana glanced at the warlock's fresh grave. A soft breeze ruffled the flowers mounded there. Roses, peonies, lilacs, lilies . . . But the scent that came to her was a powerful essence of peppermint and thyme. Karsh's scent.

The pain of loneliness and loss stabbed Ileana anew. She pictured him dying in the woods of Salem. Bleeding from the rocks her idiot cousins, Tsuris and Vey, had thrown. She heard again his last gasped words: "It is written. All is written."

With an aching emptiness, the bereaved witch returned to Karsh's writings. And found the beginning of an answer.

After the hanging, the widow's three children were scattered, given to "righteous" witch-fearing families who "cleansed their souls through toil." In other words, dear Ileana, three little ones who had known only generosity, kindness, and love were put to work as servants in the households of people who hated their kind.

The family who took in Abigail's oldest son was named Hazlitt — this child whose true clan was Antayus. But more of this later.

Later?! A bit of the fiery old Ileana awoke. *Merciless trickster,* she felt like shouting at the grave, where now the flowers fluttered as if chuckling. *Impatient fledgling,* she could imagine Karsh silencing her. With a sigh, she turned the page.

Abigail's eldest son, a boy of eight when he was orphaned, vowed at eighteen that the DuBaer family would suffer as his own had. With his brother and sister, he cast a powerful spell.

A pledge.

A curse.

That in every generation, an Antayus would cause the death of a DuBaer son. The boy was driven by misery and anger, but the curse has stood through time. No generation has been spared. . . .

"Ileana?"

The witch looked up, doubly startled by what she had just read *and* by the unexpected presence of Miranda DuBaer.

Quickly shutting Karsh's journal, Ileana scrambled to her feet. "Where's your keeper?" she rudely asked, looking for Thantos.

Miranda's gray eyes, so like Ileana's, so like the twins', registered hurt, but her smile held steady. "I am alone. Are you angry with me?"

Surprised by Miranda's directness, Ileana's impulse was to deny that anything was wrong, to lie and say, "Of course not."

"I know you're disappointed with me," Miranda added. "But are you also angry?"

"Yes," Ileana owned. "I don't understand you. I don't know you anymore. When I did, when I was a child, you were the most protective and loving woman I'd ever met. I wanted to be just like you. I dreamed that you were my real and secret mother —"

"I loved you very much, Ileana," Miranda interrupted. "When Beatrice died in childbirth, I tried to take her place."

"Well, it seems you have. I mean, you're practically married to my father, aren't you?"

"Ileana!" This time Miranda's smile did disappear.

"Your daughters arrived here yesterday, and you've made no attempt to spend time with them. You know I'm . . ." It was hard for Ileana to admit it, but she forced herself. "I'm not well. My powers seem to have . . . diminished . . . quite a lot. I'm in no condition to guide and protect them."

"I know," Miranda said gently. "And I . . ." Ileana caught Miranda's jumbled thoughts: *And I am diminished, too. My powers. My heart. I was afraid —*

"Afraid of what?" Ileana demanded.

Shaken, Miranda reached out to take Ileana's hand, but the younger witch refused, spitefully crossing her arms. "Afraid that I am useless, worse than useless to them."

"Worse than useless?" Ileana scoffed, thinking of her own powerless state. "What could be worse than useless?"

"Dangerous," Miranda murmured, then quickly changed the subject. "As for getting to know them . . . my . . . the twins, I was just on my way to your cottage. That's where the twins are staying, isn't it?"

"Yes, but you've taken the long way around, haven't you? This cemetery, the Antayus Cemetery, so different from the lavish park where your husband and parents are buried, isn't exactly on your way. Or did you come to pray over Karsh?"

"That was one reason," Miranda answered. "The other is, I thought I might find you here."

Ileana realized Miranda had more to say and waited.

With a deep sigh, Miranda faced her. "I am tired," she said, her beautiful eyes beginning to brim with tears. "Tired of sorrow, secrets, and curses."

"Curses?" Ileana asked cautiously.

"The Antayus Curse," Miranda confirmed.

That Aron's sheltered widow had known all along what Karsh had only entrusted to Ileana after his death was painful.

Miranda saying it out loud rattled Ileana and made crystal clear the meaning of what she'd just read. Beatrice had been a Hazlitt. The Hazlitts were one of the three

75

families that gave their names to Abigail's children. Beatrice Hazlitt was of the Antayus clan.

Leila DuBaer, Ileana's shrewd grandmother, must have known. And been afraid that Beatrice would carry out the curse. That was what Leila had objected to. Not Beatrice's lowly birth, but her dangerous heredity. That was why Leila had tried to convince her son not to marry Beatrice. She did not hate Ileana's mother, she feared her.

Miranda intercepted the younger witch's troubled thoughts. "Yes, yes," she cried. "That's it exactly. And I witnessed it. I saw how Beatrice was treated — scorned, derided. I pitied and defended her."

Too many revelations. Ileana's head began to swim. She was drowning in them.

"I was on my way to your cottage," Miranda now said, "to extend an invitation . . . to dinner at Crailmore tomorrow, a family dinner, Ileana," she hurried on before the surprised young witch could angrily refuse. "I hope . . . no, I urge you to accept. The twins deserve a chance to know their heritage, to see Crailmore for themselves. They will need your help and encouragement. It is your ancestral home, too, Ileana, the place where your mother lived —"

"And died," Ileana interrupted.

Ileana glanced at Beatrice's simple grave, at the lilac sprig she'd left on the tarnished bronze plaque. Only then, seeing the pale blossom awash in the scarlet blaze of sunset, did she realize how late in the day it was.

After a moment, her sullen frown faded and her head cleared. "Of course I'll go," she told Miranda, suddenly elated at the idea of carrying Beatrice's fearsome legacy, the Antayus Curse, back into the DuBaer fortress.

CHAPTER EIGHT
A WARNING IN THE NIGHT

"Did you hear that?" Alex woke with a start and poked at her sleeping sister.

Someone was in the hallway just outside the bedroom. Was it Ileana? Home after all? Alex started to relax.

Then she heard whispers. Cackling giggles.

Outside, more footsteps — among them the strange, unsteady loping of a four-footed creature, a wobbly beast with paws like a cat. Boris? No, this thing was bigger, heavier, and struggling for balance.

Whoever was in the house was not Ileana.

Whatever was outside was not a pet.

A sickening stench wafted through the open window. Like rancid, wet cat fur had been sprayed with aftershave. Alex almost hurled.

"Cam," Alex whispered urgently, leaning over and shaking her twin. "Wake up! Someone's here."

Cam burrowed under her pillow and swatted Alex away.

The twins were wiped. The last eight days had been a full-on shock-o-rama and it had taken a major toll on them. When Cam returned from seeing Jason off, she'd found Alex fast asleep on Ileana's deluxe, double-king-sized, goddess-worthy bed. She hadn't had the heart or the energy to wake her twin, even to tell her about Jason — or the wooden sign she'd found on her walk with Shane. She'd barely dragged herself to the bed.

Now Alex was shaking her.

"What?" Cam said groggily. "Go away, I'm sleeping."

Someone's in the — Alex started to telegraph.

She didn't have to finish. In a flash, Cam bolted upright and whirled to face the window. She grabbed Alex's hand. Breathing rapidly, she blurted, "It hurts! It needs us!"

"What? What needs us? What do you see, Cami? Are you having a vision?"

"No, more like a dream. Of eyes — just eyes, eyes with long dark lashes, floating in the air. Alex, I know those eyes."

Alex was afraid to ask. "Whose eyes?"

"I'm not sure. But I've seen them before. Some . . . animal. Or person. It's trying to find us. It's wounded. And it's scared." She swallowed. "What's out there, Als?"

Alex didn't get a chance to answer. A thunderous roar rocked the room. The unsteady footsteps she'd heard before were sprinting now toward the cottage. Its paws were pounding the earth, as if it were about to blast right through the window and attack!

"Run!" Cam screamed. "It's coming."

They raced toward the door and then crashed into each other, stopping short at the exact same sound — sickening, terrifying, and unmistakable: the screaming of a creature in excruciating pain.

Fast as she and Cam were, Alex knew they would not see it. It had turned away already. She could hear it darting back through the bushes, the sound of its aching roar fading as it ran away.

Their own terror up-ticked as they started after it. The moment they rushed out the bedroom door, Cam slid, skidded.

A circle of something gritty — soil, gravel, sand? — was on the floor. It trailed from Ileana's bedroom down the long hallway and led straight into the sitting room. The scent was familiar to Alex, from Ileana's garden. Night-shade? Jimson weed? Nettle? She couldn't remember which one had smelled this way. All she knew was . . .

Cam knelt and picked up some of the coarse powder, rubbing it between her thumb and fingers, about to inhale the grains

. . . it was toxic! "Stop!" Alex shouted, sweeping the particles from her sister's hand. "It's a poisonous herb. I can't remember which one but —"

"— it's connected to whatever just happened," Cam finished Alex's sentence.

"As you would say —" Alex clenched her jaw and strode toward the front door where the "trail" ended. "Duh."

"Someone was trying to lure us outside." Cam ignored Alex's knee-jerk diss. "Unless this was meant for Ileana."

Alex's hand froze on the doorknob.

Her twin's momentary paralysis pushed Cam forward. Opening the front door, she seized Alex's arm and they stepped outside together.

Strange scents mingled in the dark, as confusing as they were frightening. The bittersweet poison of deadly nightshade and, again, the putrid musk of damp fur and stinging aftershave. And another odor, a new and scary scent hard to identify.

Alex heard Cam gasp. She turned to see her sister staring at Ileana's front lawn, her phenomenal eyes cutting through the darkness.

"What?" Alex whispered, shivering. "I smell it, but I can't see it. What is it?"

A wooden post had been set into the lawn. Attached to the top was a scrap of yellow cloth. Its edges were ragged, as if it had been torn from a larger piece of fabric. On it, crudely smeared in bright red, was a message:

Go home while you can.

It was written in blood.

Cam choked back the scream lodged in her throat. "The watchers! They were here," she whispered, though no one was listening now, or watching. She was sure of it. "They were in the house, right outside our door. We didn't even sense them."

Alex stood motionless. Only her eyes moved from the warning message on the bloody cloth to the woods beyond. Her tone, when she finally spoke, was clipped. "We have enemies here. With their own magick."

Cam hugged herself. She was shivering.

Alex seethed, "If Tsuris and Vey did this, they are roadkill."

"Scratch that," Cam said, the shock beginning to wear off. "This is not the work of Two-Doofus, Inc."

"You're right. Whoever did this is smart and trying to show us he — or they — can scare us into leaving."

"Done deal." Cam turned and started for the cottage. "Sunrise? I'm gone."

Alex grasped Cam's elbow hard and swung her around. "No deal! Sunrise? We stay, and nail whoever did this — throw down some T'Witch power!"

Cam frowned. Her sister led with her heart, her emotions, her anger — never with her head. "Look," she said, going into Cam-rational mode, "we may be talented, or whatever they say we are, but even if we do figure out who wants us gone, we don't know enough to fight them."

Alex's jaw was set. "Then let's be quick learners, Barnes, 'cause we won't be stealthed again. We have every right to be here. We were born here!"

Cam tried to squish the thought . . .

Too late. Alex heard her. "What sign? What house? What are you thinking about?"

Half an hour later, dressed for the chilly night, they set out into the darkness. Clouds moved across the pale moon, but Cam easily retraced the path she and Shane had taken.

"You sure we're going in the right direction?" Alex asked. She was hyper, wired, skittish. The scent of the wounded animal that had almost attacked them was still in her nostrils. Anxiously, she waved her flashlight across the thick brush, wielding it like a light-saber.

"I know where it is," Cam said calmly. "I deliberately kicked it under a big rhododendron so I could find it later."

After a few minutes, Cam pointed triumphantly to a bush of dark green, shiny leaves ripe with purple flowers. Everything was as she'd left it — the tree root, the indentation of the plank in the soft earth, the scuffed imprint of Cam's fall. Even the streak of her kick was clear.

Only the board was missing.

Alex got down next to Cam and helped her rummage around under the rhododendron. "It's gone," she fumed, standing and brushing mud from the knees of her jeans. "I wonder who took it. Let's play the name game, or should I say the Shane game? Wonder-warlock obviously wanted to be sure you didn't find it again."

"It wasn't necessarily Shane," Cam contradicted, giving up the search. "It could have been . . . some animal."

"Right. Some artistic, wood-craving beaver ignored all the other branches in the forest and decided he wanted one with a weird design on it." Then Alex softened. "Okay, look, even if Shane swiped the wood, he can't hide a house. I say we find it."

"It was torn down — years ago," Cam said numbly, "according to Shane."

"Hmmm, to believe or not to believe? That is the question — not. I say we look for it. Which way?"

"Well, there are supposed to be some caves over that way." Reluctantly, Cam pointed into the darkness. "They're interconnected. I bet they lead to Crailmore."

"The DuBaer compound. Aron and Miranda probably lived nearby. And you did find the sign right over here."

Cam led the way unenthusiastically. Buried in her own thoughts, which came through loud and clear to Alex, she was all about: *But why would Shane move the sign, and why did I just* know *he was lying when he said the house had been torn down?*

"Because he has something to hide?" Alex ventured, thinking about seeing the skeeve in the arms of the black-haired witch. "Bet you're sorry now that you cut out on Karsh's funeral to get in Shane's face about —"

"Shane? You think I left the funeral because of Shane?" Cam spun to face her sister. "I already told you —" She stopped. Ooops. No, she hadn't.

"Jason?! He *followed* us — and was there at the funeral?" Alex was floored. Then she remembered b-ball boy's dash to the ticket counter when she and Cam were boarding.

 85

"Back up, why would you think my leaving the funeral had anything to do with Shane?" Now Cam was curious.

"Hello. Because of the . . . Look!" Alex's flashlight beam caught something red glinting through the trees. A dash in the mirage's direction proved it to be . . .

"A stained-glass window." Cam stopped alongside her sister and stared awestruck at the piece of crimson glass dangling from the high window of a stone tower in the middle of the woods.

Without another word, they thrashed through bramble and brush until Alex's flashlight clanged against something metallic. "It's a gate. Or was," she said, illuminating a panel of rusty wrought-iron spikes.

Cam's shoe found a second section underfoot. It was lying on a slab of cobblestones, timeworn and green with moss. Looking down at it, she saw that there was a rectangle cut out of this piece of gate exactly the shape and size of the board she'd found. She reached for Alex's hand and was met halfway by it. Together they moved along the remnants of a cobblestone path toward what they now knew stood just beyond the trees.

The path led them to a crumbling rock wall and through a stone archway buckling under a dense tangle of wild roses.

As they passed through the archway, the clouds that

had darkened the night shifted. Moonlight illuminated a breathtaking sight. Before them, a magnificent ruin reared. The remains of what had once been an imposing stone cottage, a country home easily twice the size of Ileana's LunaSoleil.

Still clutching each other's hands, Alex and Cam walked slowly toward the house. The cobblestone path disappeared as they picked their way through a bramble of overgrown weeds, flowers, and wild herbs, which had once been a lovingly cared-for garden.

Aside from the electric tingle that had shot through her the moment the house came into view, Cam was unexpectedly impressed. A clear picture hadn't formed in her mind, but she'd never imagined something as big and clearly once beautiful as this. It wasn't as showy as the estates in The Heights, Marble Bay's most exclusive district, but it definitely rivaled her home.

"It *is* your home," Alex cut in, awed. "Cam, we were born here."

Cam did feel surprisingly moved, psyched, and proud. Her eyes had begun to tear. She didn't want Alex to notice, so she turned away and pretended to be casually checking out the moonlit *casa*.

While it was easy to see how amazing the cottage must have been, up close it was clear that time had taken a fierce toll on the place. There were gaping holes in the wooden shingles of the dormers and roof. White mold dappled the rest. Ivy, out of control, strangled a dilapidated chimney, while a wisteria vine, its purple flowers dangling like bunches of grapes, its branches grown thick as arms, crushed the front of the house, blocking the front door and covering the mullioned windows.

The windows that were not closed off by nature had been boarded up; a few, high up like the broken stained-glass pane Alex had spotted, hung jagged, dangerous, and out of reach.

"No way in," Cam was about to conclude, until she noticed something that felt out of place. At the back of the house was a large mound of leaves, twigs, and rocks — a mountain, too carefully constructed to have been blown there, by wind and rain. It was covering something. Cam telescoped through the pile, then kicked away the leaves. "Alex!" she called out excitedly. "There's a cellar door — and someone's gone to a lot of trouble to keep it hidden."

"Score! You go, tracker girl!" Alex was by Cam's side in a flash. She reached over to pull the double doors open when a familiar feeling of dizziness stopped her. She knew what would follow: The ringing in her ears would mute every sound of the forest, of the night, of her sister's voice drifting toward her now from far, far away. Was Cam saying, "Wait, no . . . stop?"

88

The shrill ringing stopped abruptly. Into the gap of silence roared something frightening and familiar: someone — or something — groaning in pain, begging to be set free. The wounded beast that had raced toward Ileana's house! It seemed to be directly below her, underground. And she smelled again the noxious stench of fear, fur, and blood, which someone had tried to cover up nauseatingly with cologne.

Cam had tried to warn Alex, but she, too, was paralyzed. An icy chill swirled around her. She panted and shivered, goose bumps raised on her arms. And as always when she was about to have a vision, everything blurred, then all at once, came into sharp focus.

Cam saw a dark tunnel, thick stone walls sweating with moisture, grottoes formed into the walls. And some kind of sleek, furry animal trapped, being taunted by frightening figures.

The caves! The caves Shane had said ran under much of the island, that's what she was seeing.

The next sensation Cam felt was her twin's hand squeezing hers. The vision faded.

Unnerved, sweating in the cold darkness, Cam was ready to bolt for the second time that night. "We can't go in here," she whispered unsteadily. "That was a warning."

"And?" Alex challenged, shaking off her fear, advancing toward the doors.

"And maybe we should heed it!" Cam swallowed. "Or at least come back in the morning."

"When what? You can have the same vision in the daylight? Leave your wuss cap at the cellar door. Get a grip and help me open this."

"I'm not being a wuss!" Cam declared. "In case you're not counting, this is the second warning we got tonight!"

Alex put her hands on her hips. "Oh, please. That lame poison trail trick was a prank meant to frighten us. Big whoop. What we just experienced was a sign. Karsh taught us that. They tell us what we have to do."

"That someone needs us," Cam conceded. She did not want to be needed, not now, not here on Coventry Island. "Alex, we're not ready," she pleaded, wanting more than ever to go —

"Home." Alex finished her thought. "This is it, Cam-a-lot. Our real home. And whatever's waiting for us inside, or underneath it, ready or not — here we come."

CHAPTER NINE
LUNASOLEIL

They descended the set of rickety steps into the basement. It was pitch-black and, save for the creaking sounds they made coming down, absolutely still.

And absolutely wrong.

The house had been boarded up, left sunless, bereft, barren, abandoned. Just the shell remained, testimony to the lively, joyous haven it once had been.

So why did Alex detect a mix of ammonia and some kind of wood polish, as if it had been cleaned recently? Cam's eyes, adjusting easily to the dark, confirmed it: not a cobweb or dust ball in sight. Someone had secretly been taking care of this house, and had gone to some trouble to hide the entrance.

This basement, which might have been used for storage, was empty now. A lonely narrow staircase in the far corner led upstairs.

That, too, seemed wrong. The vision Cam had just had, the cries Alex had just heard had come from *under* the earth, not above it.

Cam scanned the wooden floor, then searched for some kind of hidden opening in the walls. Nothing so far.

She was interrupted by the sound of Alex-the-impatient bounding upstairs. In a flash, she was at the top — frozen, terrified of crossing the threshold into the main living area. Cam hurried up beside her. Together they gently opened the door.

Instantly, they were bathed in a warm, comforting, welcoming feeling. It was, Cam would describe it later, like being in a house of worship: sacred and safe, separated and protected from the outside world. Like the strong embrace of a father, the nurturing arms of a mother. This was Aron and Miranda's home.

This, according to Karsh and Ileana, was where they had been born. The vast space they were staring at now must have been a warm wonderful room. Brilliant sunlight would have streamed through the skylights and picture windows, now sadly boarded up.

In a corner was a handsome daybed of carved mahogany. Without turning to face her, Alex put an arm around her sister and they walked cautiously together toward the beautiful divan. There, beside it in a corner stood a uniquely beautiful cradle. Made of bent willow branches, it was wide enough that two infants might easily have rested on the plump cushion inside it.

Years and years ago, before memory, she and Cam had slept side by side in the beautiful handcrafted cradle.

Her heart pounding fiercely, Alex realized that the cushion was the size of the faded patchwork quilt Miranda had brought to her first meeting with them, the fragrant herb-filled quilt Alex had since worn as a shawl. Was wearing now, in fact. It was their baby blanket. Their mother had kept it with her from the day she left her beloved home fifteen years ago, believing her infant daughters were dead — until the day, just over a week ago, that she found them again.

Cam felt Alex's arm relax, as if the limb itself were sighing.

A memory came to Cam, wispy as a dream. A shadow leaning close. A tall figure with wide shoulders and thick hair, a man she could only make out vaguely, a misty silhouette. He was holding something . . . a glittering bangle of some sort. Cam's fingers moved involuntarily to her necklace. The gold amulet was warm.

"Alex?" she said.

"I know," her twin answered. "The cradle." They sat down on the daybed.

"Is your moon charm heating up?" Cam asked, her voice breaking, her throat beginning to thicken with tears.

Alex felt the amulet. *Little Artemis*, she heard a voice say. It was faraway and faint. A deep, tender voice that had spoken to her once before. *Wear this, little Artemis. It was made not only with my hands but all my heart and strength.*

Cam's hot tears washed away the image of the man and began to melt something hard and brittle that had been stuck in her chest since she and Alex stepped off the ferry. She hadn't been aware of it until this moment, until now when it was dissolving. It had felt like an iron vest. Armor. With it gone, she could breathe again. And feel Alex's arms hugging her now.

"Welcome home," her sniffling twin whispered.

Laughing through her tears, Cam returned the embrace. "Welcome home," she responded.

Artemis, she thought. Alex. The girl of a million hair colors and five defiantly shabby outfits, one of which she wore now: a denim jacket frayed at the bottom, holes randomly puncturing it. Alex — angry, rebellious, impulsive, gutsy. How could the bedraggled, bewildered Montana tough girl who'd dissed and dismissed Cam the first time they met, then showed up on her doorstep a week later, even be *related* to Camryn Barnes?

Any and all doubts Cam had ever harbored about her exact double — who was the opposite of her in every way — crumbled.

Embracing her sister, Alex was blown away by how shampoo-sweet Cam's hair smelled. Despite marching through mud, shouldering branches and bramble, Camryn Barnes was squeaky clean from top to high-end Timberland-protected toes. Cam had somehow managed to brush her hair and gather it in a scrunchie.

Spoiled suburban princess. A part of her still thought of Cam as that, Alex realized. It was the first impression she'd held onto even when she'd learned better. Despite DNA, despite everything they'd been through in the last year, Alex stubbornly clung to her uniqueness. "No one's like me!" she had declared to friends who'd dared suggest Cam looked like her twin.

That was then, before . . . All of it now wiped away like chalk dust on a blackboard.

They had shared the same cradle. In this room, they had stared up into their parents' silvery gray eyes, windows to souls that matched their own.

Camryn and Alexandra — Apolla and Artemis — didn't know how long they sat there on the daybed. Only that their hearts were beating in a steady tandem rhythm, and that they were remembering, each in her own way, the gift of the necklaces as their father first clasped them around their chubby infant necks, and of being held safely in their mother's arms, cloaked in unconditional love.

In some weird way, what Cam and Alex felt mostly — was free.

"Let's look around." Cam broke the silence. Alex only nodded. Then, wordlessly, they turned away from each other, as if that could keep the next long-buried memory from surfacing: of their mother's screams, of being taken from her, of being separated, ripped apart.

At a pace that felt like slo-mo, robotic, like swimming through Jell-O, they explored the cottage. Cam stayed downstairs and floated through the rooms, taking in everything. And nothing.

Alex was drawn up a spiral staircase with a hazardously broken railing. It led to a loft, a balcony, really, lined with shelves where candles, crystals, and books covered in undisturbed dust abounded. Whoever kept the basement clean, had not bothered up here. Two large easy chairs, also timeworn, were separated by a cedar chest.

It looked like a cozy private place where Aron and Miranda might have sat together reading, confiding in each other, or planning for the future. Alex ran her hand over a chair back and stared at the chest. Her heart quickened as she opened it.

The chest contained linens. A blend of herbal scents hit her and made her well up all over again. Sheets, blankets, pillows — each seemed bathed in its own fragrance.

Beneath the layer of linens there was a hammer, a skein of gold chain, and ingots of gleaming gold. Aron must have made their amulets from gold nuggets like these, maybe designed their pendants right here. The bottom of the chest was filled with books. The one that made Alex laugh was *What to Expect When You're Raising Twins.* Even witches needed parenting advice!

The one that piqued her interest was *The Erinyes.*

Alex began to read. "The Erinyes, more commonly known as The Furies, lived in the underworld, a place for the cursed. They were outcasts who some believed existed to punish evildoers. The Furies were unstoppable. They were usually represented as three:

Tisiphone, Megaera, and Alecto.

CHAPTER TEN
ANYTHING YOU CAN DO, I CAN DO BETTER

Late the next morning, Alex lay in bed replaying the amazing events of the last few days. Finding LunaSoleil was the high point, the most meaningful. More so for Cam, she thought. Inside their parents' home, Cam had made her first real connection to Coventry and got it: She belonged here, too.

Yet Shane had tried to prevent that from happening.

The attraction between Shane and Cam was big. But after last night?

Detraction? Bigger.

Wonder-warlock had lied to Cam about LunaSoleil.

So what else was he hiding? Alex ruffled her hair and yawned. Maybe it didn't matter. After last night, Shane had to be *so over*. Why hurt her sister even more by telling Cam that slimy Shane "forgot" to mention his snaky sweetie?

Oka-a-ay, so maybe Alex should have rethought that. A few hours later she showed up on their doorstep.

Shane's girlfriend, the violet-eyed velociraptor Alex had seen at the funeral, dramatically draped in a sweeping floor-length cape the exact pale purple color of her eyes, introduced herself as Sersee.

She came with backup, the same pair who'd been sitting with her at Karsh's service. The shorter one, in an emerald-green cloak, looked like Peter Pan gone punk. A feathery cap of wispy light brown hair barely skimmed the pixie's neck, around which a barbed-wire necklace was tattooed. Arms crossed insolently, she said, "I'm Michaelina."

The lumbering, lumpy one in an ill-fitting faded rose cloak was Epie.

Alex disliked them instantly. The snotty remarks directed at Cam and herself during Karsh's funeral had come from this trash-talking trio — *a crone and her cronies,* she couldn't help thinking.

"If we're the crones," Sersee smiled mischievously,

"what does that make you — crone-wannabes? Or is it crona-bes? Crone-clones, perhaps?"

Ooops. They were mind readers, at least this one was. Quickly, Alex lobbed back, "Is this just a drive-by insult-fest, or should we get the Scrabble set out? How long are you planning to stay?"

Portly Epie stifled a giggle.

Sersee shot daggers at her, then eyed Cam. "Is the evil spawn of Ozzy Osbourne always this rude?"

"Only when there's a good reason," Cam shot back breezily. She didn't know these girls, but something had Alex in diss-mode. She'd back up her sister up.

Sersee's nostrils flared. "Let's start again. We were so impressed with your inspiring tributes at the funeral of dear Lord Karsh, we wanted to meet you."

"Color us met." Alex started to turn away, but Cam, curious now, stopped her.

"Besides," Sersee continued, motioning to the blood-stained message still visible on the yellow patch of fabric, "we wouldn't want you to get the impression that you're not wanted here. Some of us really hope you stay. For a bit."

Surprised, Cam's eyes widened while Alex's narrowed suspiciously.

Sersee continued. "We wanted to find out if the DuBaer twins of legend were as . . . special . . . as we've always been told."

"Special in what way?" Cam wanted to know.

"Why, in every way," the young witch crooned, beginning to walk away from them toward the water. "Come with me?" she invited.

Cam did. Alex grudgingly followed.

"For instance," Sersee said when the great lake was in view, "we've heard your powers are very precious, and we'd —"

Precocious, Michaelina silently corrected the spokeswitch. *Means unusually gifted, talented.*

She's right, Sers, Epie hesitantly offered.

How very precocious *of you*, Sersee snarled at her lackeys. Then she realized with dismay that Alex had intercepted the unspoken exchange. *Of course I meant precious,* she sent back, then scrambled the next part of her message, which turned Epie white with fright.

That got Alex's attention. Sersee, it seemed, could easily block her from reading her vicious mind. Could she and Cam bar Sersee's from theirs? Not so far. Advantage Sersee.

Cam's attention had been drawn, now that they'd reached the shoreline, to a cluster of cliffs miles up the coast and shrouded in mist. Her zoom-lens vision revealed the top of a tower behind the cloudy veil. It must be the tallest structure on the island, she thought. Before she could censor herself, she blurted, "That tower in the distance — is that part of Crailmore?"

Oozing with phony sympathy, Sersee cooed, "You haven't been there yet? To your own ancestral home? Isn't your . . . beloved mother there?"

Snap! Her tone changed to withering as she made the universal circle-around-the-ear symbol for cuckoo. "Oh, wait, I forgot — Mom's bonkers!"

Alex lunged for her, but Cam swiftly stepped between them. "If you're talking about Miranda DuBaer," she warned, "bad-mouthing her is so *not* the way to go. She's three times as powerful as when she left."

Epie's chunky forehead crinkled. "How do you figure?"

"Do the math —" Cam started.

"She's got us now," Alex finished.

Sersee took a step back. "Ooooh, I'm so scared. Let's see, how did you put it? Color me warned?" she mocked, trying to stare Alex down. She picked the twin least likely to blink.

Michaelina broke the impasse. "So, will you be training for your initiation here?"

Their initiation. Ileana had alluded to it several times but had told them little. They assumed it was a ceremony promoting them to full-fledged witches or something.

Epie piped up, "Who'll be preparing you now that Karsh is dead as a doornail?"

Cam blanched at blabber-witch's tact-free bluntness.

"Not Ileana," Sersee sniped. "Another basket case."

Eyes flashing, Alex was again ready to pummel the leader of the attack-pack. "We're as ready as we need to be."

From the corner of her eye, Cam noticed Michaelina's sly grin. Sersee tapped her chin. "Really? Why don't we find out?"

Alex folded her arms and leaned back on a tall boulder, unafraid.

They started with telekinesis. Epie demonstrated. She pointed to a black seashell on the rocky shore and closed her eyes. The shell began to rise and, as if it had turned into a Frisbee, went wheeling into the great lake, hitting the water with a loud splash.

Alex stayed put. Even from this distance, she could outdo that lame exhibition. She focused on a bunch of shells. They skimmed the lake, leapfrogging, leaving a series of ripples in the water.

Sersee rolled her eyes. "Bragging rights to Telekinesis 101 go to Alex. Let's move on." She summoned the pixie witch and pointed to a dot on the horizon. "Michaelina, that boat out there — who's on it?"

Michaelina trained binocular eyes out to sea. She smiled. "It's the ferry. Our brave Captain Bump Blubberhead is on his way back to the mainland." Mischievously, she cocked her head. "He doesn't know about the approaching bad weather. Unfortunate, isn't it?"

Before the twins could stop her, Michaelina conjured up a violent — very localized! — storm. Buckets of rain gushed from the sky, as if a dam had burst right above the boat. The wind whipped fiercely, and the ferry pitched violently. At any moment, it would capsize. Its lone captain, caught unaware, went flying backward, then forward, then sideways like a pinball bumping against the sides of the boat. Surely, he would go over with the next toss of the boat.

Only . . . not. His eyes widened, his jaw slackened, he keeled forward — then, stopped, as if the plug of the pinball machine had been suddenly pulled out. He'd stopped dead, but stayed alive aboard his vessel and rode out the "storm."

"You almost went overboard with that one," Cam deadpanned.

"What did you do?" Epie was bewildered.

Sersee sneered, "The Sun Queen blinded him, stunned him into stopping in his tracks."

"Coo —" Epie started but thought better of it.

Michaelina stepped back, a look of alarm — or was it awe? — on her face.

"Let's pick up the pace," Sersee commanded, frustrated that the one-ups were backfiring. She decided to make it personal. She pointed at Cam's head and conjured up a spell. The scrunchie holding back Cam's hair slid off. Startled, Cam felt her shiny, silky shoulder-length tresses kink up and fly wildly in all directions, coarse, bristly, like she'd put her finger in an electric socket.

"Bad hair day, Princess?" Sersee mocked her.

Red-faced, Cam quickly tied her bristly, bushy hair back. Then she got angry. She was all set to see how Sersee liked barbecued curls, when Alex got in the way. Alex, who'd always given better than she got, beat her sister to the get-even punch.

"Hey, bony macaroni," she taunted tall, skinny Sersee. "What's *up* with your cloak?" Telekinetically, Alex tossed the purple cape into the air. Still fastened around Sersee's neck, it swirled wildly, battering the startled witch's face. It looked like a cyclone wrapping itself like a turban around her head.

Sersee's sputtering rage was muted inside the churning garment. Struggling to hide a grin, Michaelina leaped forward to help her frantic friend peel off the stifling cloak.

"Yeeew, cape hair!" Epie shrieked, pointing at her leader, whose black curls had been mashed into a soaring point, a hairy Leaning Tower of Pisa, a witch's hat without a brim — or a dunce cap.

"Not to split hairs," Alex mocked, "but the cone-head look is so five centuries ago."

Sersee undid the drawstring tie, gasping for breath.

"Okay," she growled, tearing her velvet cape from Michaelina's hands and tossing it down like soiled laundry. "So you can toy with telekinesis. Point taken. Now how about transmutation?"

"Only trackers can transmutate," Epie proudly announced. "Trackers and Sersee."

"We'll see what you can really do." Blazing eyes fastened on the twins, Sersee ignored her lackey. "Or, can't."

Beads of perspiration popped out on Cam's forehead. *Alex! We don't know how to do this. What if she —*

Her twin remained calm. *We'll figure it out. Don't let her see you sweat.*

Sersee knelt at water's edge and recited a short incantation. She dug into the wet sand along the shoreline and came up with a bumpy-skinned green bullfrog about the size of a grapefruit. "Ribbit, ribbit," it croaked innocently.

What was she going to do to it? Cam shuddered.

Sersee wrapped her clawlike fingers around the slippery creature, preventing it from leaping away. Shooting a savage smile at Cam and Alex, she said, "This transmutation spell is done silently — a little secret between me and . . . Kermit here. Oh, and if you feel the urge to try and stop me? Don't. Because you can't! So sit back, watch, and be awestruck!"

Alex sucked in a sharp breath.

Sersee did not even move her lips as she stared at her prey. Slowly, horrifically, the frog's legs began to fold into its belly. Its buggy eyes, bulging with terror, had started to sink into its head. Sersee was turning the frog into something that wasn't alive.

"You'll kill it!" Cam shouted. "Alex, move it away from her!"

As she'd been warned, Alex could do nothing to stop her. Sersee's magick was strong, and fun-time was over. It was all about life and death now.

Frantically looking for something to stop the vicious witch, Cam came up empty. Until . . . was it possible? Michaelina's lips were moving. Was she mouthing Sersee's spell? She nudged Alex, who took the hint, and was horrified at what she heard.

> *Dark magick that poisons the night,*
> *Thundering clouds that block out the light.*
> *Take this creature as I command!*
> *Turn it to wood, dead and peeling, this I demand.*
> *From frog to log, and if this be mean?*
> *Hey, he said it himself, "It ain't easy bein' green!"*

Sersee cracked up at her own sick joke. The bullfrog's healthy green hue faded to rotted brown, its rounded body elongated, its bumpy scales broke out into rough bark. Cruelly, Sersee had left its eyes bugging out of the end of what was now a dead log. Triumphantly, she raised it before Cam and Alex like a sword. "Transmutation! Witness the power."

"Witness this," Alex snarled, grasping her moon necklace.

Michaelina had accidentally gone all snitch-witch, giving them a clue. Was it enough to help them save the innocent creature?

Cam snatched the log from Sersee and cradled it in her arm, prompting witch-superior to chortle, "Are you going to rock it to sleep? It's already comatose, or didn't you notice!"

Cam ignored her, clutched her sun charm, and together with Alex did the only thing they could think of. They recited the same spell Sersee had, substituting good magick for bad, mercy for cruelty.

Let this work, let this work, Cam prayed, closing her eyes.

It will. It has to, Alex responded, though she had no idea if it would.

But when their necklaces heated up, straining toward each other to fit together like magnets, the T'Witches knew they'd done it. The powerful magick inside them — though they hadn't been taught how to use it — somehow had prevailed.

Alex heard it first. A low, throaty, "Ribbit! Ribbit!"

Cam felt the log moving, constricting, curling into a slippery bumpy ball as the frog once again took its own color and form. Very much alive, it pounced itself out of Cam's arms and splashed into the sea.

Steam was practically coming out of Sersee's ears.

Of course, Alex had to rub it in. "Say thank you, Sersee, your PETA membership card is in the mail."

Cam high-fived her sister.

"Not so fast," Sersee snarled and snapped her fingers. Out of the woods, a sleek black panther materialized. It wore a studded dog collar, from which a round orange tag hung. "Heel!" she ordered. The animal paused, looked curiously at Cam, then sat at Sersee's feet.

"This is my new pet," she cooed malevolently. "A panther. He follows me everywhere!"

Alex started to cough. The smell assaulted her, that same hideous mix of aftershave and cat fur she'd nearly choked on last night. "Your pet needs a bath," she managed to say between coughing spasms.

Its eyes, dark as night, fascinated and terrified Cam. They were the eyes she'd seen floating outside her window last night. Framed by long, thick black eyelashes.

"What are you going to do to it?" Cam demanded.

"Do?" Sersee's face had darkened. "Trust me, the damage is already done."

"It's terrified," Cam couldn't stop herself. "It's hurting."

"You think?" Sersee stroked its head. "Well, he did have a little accident last night. He got cut running through the woods. Lost a lot of blood, I think."

Cam's eyes widened. It was them! *They* were at the house with that panther thing!

Then it hit her *hard*. They'd been following her. *They* were the watchers,

Alex grimaced. The poison herbs, the blood! For all their T'Witch power, they'd never heard, seen, nor sensed a thing, not until Sersee had "summoned them," purposely woken them up.

No way they could do all that on their own, Alex thought angrily. They weren't that good. They so had help. She blurted, "Kudos on last night's stealth attack. Did your boyfriend help plan it or just lead you to us?"

Sersee's lips curled. This was going exactly as she'd hoped. "*Boyfriend* is such a mainland label. We are so much more than that. Soul mates, in fact, destined to be together always. But you knew that, Alex, you saw us snuggling at Lord Karsh's funeral."

As if she'd just thought of it, the wily witch eyed Cam, "You know him, too. Shane Wright. He belongs to me."

Cam couldn't breathe. She felt as if her stomach had hit the ground. Slowly, she turned to her sister and spoke with her eyes: You *knew*. You didn't tell me! How could you?

Furious, Cam spun and stomped away. She didn't get far before Sersee shouted, "Wait! Don't you even want to know my pet's name?"

"Not really," Cam shouted back without turning her head.

"No? But I think you'll like it." Sersee yelled at Cam's back, "It's Jason."

CHAPTER ELEVEN
DOUBLE-CROSSED

Fear struck like a hammer. Cam ran wildly, trampling bramble, thrusting aside tangles of branches — reckless motion to keep her imagination from running wild.

Jason?

Panting, she refused to even allow the grotesque thought in. No way! She would *not go* there. Only, she did.

But not until she'd gotten back to Ileana's, noticed the dinner invitation to Crailmore, with Ileana's scrawled message: *Pick you up at six. Be ready!* Not until she'd showered and double-shampooed to get Sersee's frizz-curse out of her hair.

Only then did Cam try to logic it all out.

Sersee had named that vile-smelling panther Jason. Coincidence? As if. The reedy crone had been *way* too eager to share that with Cam.

Sick joke? Like the poison herbs and blood message on the yellow fabric — yellow like Jason's tennis shirt?

Could be . . . but why? What did Sersee and her little horde of horror-ettes have against them? Simple jealousy? All Shane had done was show her around Coventry. Sersee had to know that — she'd been spying on them the whole time!

Again, those eyes loomed in front of her. Panther's eyes. Jason's eyes.

Eeww! Cam shook her head hard, as if she could shake out the too weird and sickening thought. No. It was a vicious trick to freak her out.

Sersee, the wicked witch of Wisconsin. Jason, the sweet cool breeze from Massachusetts. One here. One *not* here. They didn't even know each other . . .

Unless, Alex had mentioned him . . .

Alex. Who'd known about the "soul mate" and hadn't bothered to share. Or what, conveniently forgot to mention, "Oh, BTW: Shane? Not single. Girlfriend, possessive, potentially evil."

Which witch was playing Cam now?

She'd brushed her hair dry and changed for dinner when she heard someone coming.

Alex . . . and she wasn't alone! Her psycho sister had brought home one of the vicious vipers, Michaelina.

Cam T-mailed Alex: *I don't want to talk to you.* Then she slipped out Ileana's back door.

Alex's mental memo replied, *You have to trust me.*

Have to? she responded. *Trust this: No way.*

Trust your instincts, Karsh had told her.

Trust your heart. That one came from Emily when Cam was only nine. "But what if your heart tells you two different things?" Cam had asked, torn between wanting to show her mom the amazing things she could do and knowing, somehow, that she shouldn't confide in Emily.

"Listen harder." Her mom had kissed the top of her head then.

Beyond the herb garden, in the woods behind the house, Cam spotted a hammock. She stretched out on it and stared up through the lacy canopy of leaves into a sapphire sky.

Go home, her gloomy heart was saying, to the parents who raised you, to Dylan, to your friends. Her friends! None of whom would keep a secret like the Shane/Sersee alliance from her! If only her cell phone worked — or if there were any phones here in the land beyond Amish. Beth was her level-headed, loyal BFF. Cam needed a dose of her reasonable perspective now.

"How is Beth, anyway? I haven't seen her since my

trip to Marble Bay." Startled, Cam twisted around so suddenly, she nearly tumbled out of the hammock. Shane saved her. Shane, whose eyes twinkled like sapphires, the exact same shade as the cloudless sky.

Minus his cape, Shane was in mainland garb: jeans and an ab-hugging, short-sleeved black T-shirt. What was this? Casual Friday on Coventry?

In spite of herself, Cam felt her tummy do the flip-flop thing. He was *so* hot, she felt her anger melting. Unfair use of cute!

She forced a picture of Sersee into her head, tried to imagine them cooing and cuddling at Karsh's funeral.

Coolly, she said, "Beth is fine. Better since she'll never see you again."

"Is that her opinion or yours? Why are you angry at me?"

"I have this quirk," Cam said. "I don't react well to liars. And, I don't like being played for a fool."

His smooth, warm hands locked over hers, and electricity shot up her body. Gently, he eased her off the hammock and into his arms. Resistance was futile. Confusion, total. Her head nestled on his chest, Cam could hear his heart beating.

"What's going on? You can tell me," he murmured, stroking her hair.

Flashback! Jason had said the same thing only two

days ago. It felt like two years ago. She didn't want the truth to sink in, not right then. But it did. She could always trust Jason. Shane — whose arms felt so good around her? Not so much. *Not at all,* Alex would have clarified.

"You lied to me," she managed to squeak out. "My parents' home wasn't torn down."

Shane seemed to stop breathing for a moment. "I'm sorry. But when you found the signpost, I knew you'd try to find the house. I didn't want you to see LunaSoleil like that — boarded up, neglected, moldy, no way to get inside. I thought you'd be devastated. I was trying to spare you."

Shane's embrace quickened her heart, but it didn't soften her brain. She would reveal no more. With effort, she pulled away. "Were you also 'sparing me' by not mentioning Sersee?"

Shane cocked his head and half-smiled. "That's what this chill is about?" He gave Cam's shoulder a reassuring squeeze. "Listen, I know she tells people I'm her boyfriend —"

"Property," Cam interrupted. "She says you belong to her, you two are soul mates."

"No way, we're not even serious," he scoffed. "I know her from school, and when I got kicked out of my house, she let me . . . she found a place for me to live.

So I'm grateful, but I don't have those kinds of feelings for her."

"What kind of feelings would those be?" Even as she hated herself for doing it, Cam flirted.

"The kind I could have . . ." He brushed a stray lock of hair off her forehead and tucked it behind her ear. ". . . Maybe one day . . . for you."

He'd done it again. She melted, wanting to believe at least this much was true. It was possible Shane had put a spell on her. Only she knew, by her instincts and in her heart, he had not.

There were two reasons Alex hadn't followed Cam home after Sersee's panther parade. Sersee and her lap-dogs were more than just mean-spirited rivals. They were dangerous.

Which led her to wonder, reason two, why Michaelina had been mouthing the words to the frog-to-log spell. And whether the punk pixie had "accidentally on purpose" given them the means to reverse the curse? Alex had more to gain hanging with the teen trio than sprinting after her shaken sister.

So, doing her best imitation of a wicked witch wanna-be — which included releasing Skeletor's hair from its towering cone-head 'do — she stayed behind to schmooze with the teen trio.

Alex didn't have to keep up the ruse for long.

Sersee got bored soon enough. With a toss of her restored, waist-length, corkscrew curls and a wave of her slinky arm, she whirled theatrically, "Errands to run, spells to cast, so many lives to ruin, so little time . . ."

Epie shrugged, curled her fingers around the panther's collar, and trotted after her.

Michaelina waited, studying Alex with open curiosity. Then, turning toward the lake and casually skimming a stone across its surface, she asked, "So what's it like where you live?"

"Ileana's cottage?" Alex said, knowing that wasn't what the pint-sized witch meant. "It's fabulous, just like her. Come on, I'll show you around."

Too cool to confess she'd meant their mainland home, Michaelina shrugged and said, "Okay. I'm open."

She was anything but.

Pumping Michaelina for info didn't yield much — except for one heart-stopping detail. She, Sersee, and Epie, best friends, called themselves The Furies.

Treading carefully, Alex asked, "Random choice of name? Or —"

Proudly, Michaelina said, "You've never heard of The Furies of legend?"

Alex had just read about them in the book stored in her parents' cedar chest. She said, "But that legend says they're outcasts, living underground, doling out punishment."

Impressed, Michaelina explained, "We're more like an updated version. Only the old-fashioned, narrow-minded," she bragged, "considered them outcasts, when really they were forward-thinkers, rebels even."

"Rebelling against what exactly?" Alex asked.

"All the junk that's shoved down our throats, Sersee says, at school and Unity Council meetings. The lore, the legends, the icky sweet kindness. Sersee says we question authority. We're deciding for ourselves what to believe."

Alex ventured, "You mean using your skills — your magick — for things other than the good of humankind?"

Michaelina chuckled. "You sound like a textbook. You sure you didn't grow up here?"

"Very," Alex confirmed as they approached the cottag. She felt Cam's confusion, and then anger, radiating through the closed front door. *Trust me*, she tried to tell her twin, but Cam sent back a sarcastic *No way* and slipped out the back door as Alex led Michaelina inside. "But I know what Lord Karsh . . ." Her throat caught. "What he taught us. The reason we have these gifts is to help."

"*You* inherited them," Michaelina pointed out. "You, of the revered DuBaer family. They don't want us to know. But the truth is, not all your famous relatives were quite so perfect."

Alex flashed on Thantos. And Fredo . . . and Tsuris and Vey. She was not surprised when Michaelina continued, "Sersee says some DuBaers were less grand and giving than others. Some helped themselves before helping anyone else." She surveyed Ileana's posh living room. "Sersee says your own guardian has probably cast a spell or two for personal gain."

Alex refrained from a knee-jerk defense of Ileana. She had been tempted herself to use her skills to, uh, "help herself" on a test, or find out what one of Cam's superficial friends was really thinking. But it would never occur to her to use her gifts to hurt an innocent person or creature.

Michaelina prodded, "Have you ever asked yourself why you just blindly believed everything Karsh taught you? Never even questioned it?"

Alex bristled. "Lord Karsh, okay? And no, I never questioned it." She didn't explain that Sara, on her deathbed, implored Alex, "Listen to him. He might look scary, but he's good."

"You guys are so touchy." Michaelina shrugged. "I meant no disrespect."

Alex continued, "And I might not have understood everything, but I knew Lord Karsh's heart. He was just everything . . . everything that was pure and wise and kind . . . and good. He protected us, guided us, loved us. I knew him." She fought back tears, which startled her almost as much as it did Michaelina. "And trying to be a fraction of the person he was, is a worthy goal."

The wiry witch's expression softened. "Well, Sersee says —" she began lamely. Then shook her head. "Oh, never mind."

"Did you ever question what *Sersee* says?" Alex asked gently.

Michaelina didn't answer. She didn't have to. And Alex didn't have to break into her head to know: Michaelina wasn't lamebrained, of course she had. But never as much as she was questioning it right now.

Or not.

Michaelina hung at Ileana's cottage just long enough to gather some juicy info. She wasted no time scooting back to Sersee, reporting word for word what she'd overheard. How respectful of Alex not to eavesdrop on the little backyard drama between Cam and Shane. Michaelina had not been so respectful. She parroted back to Sersee, "We're not that serious. I don't have those kinds of feelings for her."

Sersee was burning up. How dare Shane tell this . . . this . . . nothing! that they weren't "that serious." Had Cam put a spell on him? Was this DuBaer princess capable of even doing that? If Sersee had been jealous before, she'd just racheted up to murderous: Cam would live just long enough to regret it.

What Sersee had seen earlier in the day added fear to her fury. On their own, Camryn and Alexandra were powerful forces not to be underestimated. Together, they were truly awesome, possibly unbeatable. Imagine figuring out how to undo the transmutation spell before they'd even been taught it, let alone initiated!

Separating them was the only option. Wasn't it lucky, then, that she knew just how to do that?

CHAPTER TWELVE
THE VOW

Ileana was back.

Or so she told herself, studying her image in the cloudy mirror propped on Karsh's fireplace mantel.

It wasn't as if she were feeling like her old self again. That would be too much to hope for. She might never *be* her old self again. The spell-casting, transmutating, incantation-chanting ingenue might be gone for good — buh-*bye* — but Ileana, dressed to kill, was back with a vengeance.

Her makeup was perfect, her blond hair brushed to shimmering brilliance, her bloodred nail polish looked eerily liquid as she tapped her fingers on the cover of Karsh's journal.

And she was wearing the diamond earrings that Thantos had given Beatrice as an engagement gift, earrings that Karsh had kept for her — along with the secret of who her father was.

Now she knew. And knew how he must fear her, fear her mother's blood. That was why he'd sent her away, given her to Karsh to raise, kept her at a "safe" distance all her life.

Only no DuBaer son was safe, not while there were Antayuses in their midst. After all, the Antayus Curse had never skipped a generation. Or so Karsh had written.

Even her old friends, impatience and glee, had returned for the occasion. She could hardly wait to lead Cam and Alex into her father's fortress.

Ileana whirled away from the mirror. She'd spent a good part of the afternoon getting ready for this evening. To that end, more important than her makeup and clothing, had been reading Karsh's journal.

You have met your grandmother Leila, met her in spirit, which I assure you is but a pale imitation of her fierceness in life, Ileana had read. *Had she been less determined, the curse might have ended.*

Your grandfather, Nathaniel, and I had devised a means for it to end. We were only boys when we came up with our plan. But as there is genius in simplicity so

simple, children may find solutions that evade their complicated elders.

Nate and I met preparing for our coming-of-age celebration, our initiation. We were fifteen, Camryn and Alexandra's age as I write this. Nathaniel DuBaer was an only child, the only living male DuBaer on Coventry Island. And I, also an only child, was the last male Antayus of my generation.

Nate lived on the northern cliffs of the island at Crailmore. My parents' home, Harbor Haven, was south of where my cottage now stands, on the leeward side of Coventry. If we'd laid eyes on each other before, neither of us recalled it. But we could remember in detail every moment of our first day together.

We were introduced by our guardians — Cristof was mine, Gentian was Nate's. Both old warlocks knew what we did not and tried to discourage our friend-ship. But something stronger drew us together. Back then, I thought it was admiration, the promise of ad-venture, the excitement of finding a high-spirited equal. Too late I learned that it was fate.

From the first day of our training, a remarkable friendship grew between Nathaniel DuBaer and me. Each of us felt we'd known the other forever. We could talk and joke easily, were equally good at most events, *could hear each other's thoughts as clearly as if we'd spoken aloud, and often knew in advance what the other was thinking.*

In casting and creating spells, summoning spirits, using concentration and telekinesis to move objects at a distance and even to pick up small creatures and move them out of harm's way, we were evenly matched. Showing off, we knotted snakes without touching them, caused snails to speed past trotting ponies, and cats to happily ride the backs of dolphins. Nate once willed my ears to flap while I made his thick, dark hair stand on end with a focused glance. In some areas, we excelled individually. My hearing was far more honed than Nate's; his ability to find hidden objects was keener than mine. Separately or combining our talents, no one could touch us in any category.

When we learned of the curse — which was shortly after our initiation ceremony — we were undaunted, idiotically unafraid, arrogant. Our solution, our pitifully childish response to a blood curse that had succeeded for two centuries and six generations, was that it would end with us. We would not marry, not father children, and so there would be no sons to kill. And since we would never kill each other, in fact, had pledged to protect each other, the curse, we reasoned, would end.

Enter Leila. Leila and her best friend, Rhianna Noble. Of all the young witches of Coventry, they were the brightest, the most powerful, and the most attractive. Yes, dear goddess mine, the one you called "Lady Potato" when you were a disrespectful child, was the most sought-after girl on Coventry Island, second only to the glamorous and willful Leila Tavisham. What Leila lacked in soft beauty, she more than made up for in brains, personality, and determination. She literally swept Nate off his feet.

We were in the square one evening walking past an outdoor café at which the young witches were having tea. Rhianna, who I knew and liked well, waved, inviting us to join them. But Nate was deep in conversation and paid no attention. I smiled and shrugged, as if to tell the girls, "Well, another time, maybe."

Then Leila's hand fluttered. A fledgling might have mistaken it for a dainty gesture of farewell, but I knew at once that it was a spell-casting gesture, an undulating wave meant to direct Leila's wishes toward her victim.

Before I could say a word, Nathaniel went down. His lanky legs grew rubbery and tangled. He gasped, pitched forward, and fell to his knees at Leila's feet.

I was about to scold the mischievous girl — and Rhianna, too, who was laughing shamelessly — when

I realized that something more than strong magick had taken place. No incantation, herb, or crystal, no flutter of a dainty hand could accomplish what had befallen Nathaniel.

When he looked up at Leila, I saw that it was too late. His clear eyes had grown foggy, his dark, fretting eyebrows had lifted. The full lips that had gasped, startled into an O, spread as slowly and sweetly as thick honey into a grin of sheer enchantment.

Nate had not just fallen because of Leila, he'd fallen for her.

Within a year, his vow never to marry was broken. I stood up for him at their wedding. And truly, Ileana, I was glad for him and for his brilliant young bride. Glad in the ignorance of youth, happy and certain that love and friendship could triumph over superstition. One vow we would not break, I told myself, to defend each other.

And it was that vow that destroyed everything.

Nathaniel and Leila had three sons, as you know. Still, I believed we could halt the curse. Thantos, the eldest, was about to turn thirteen when fate proved me wrong.

Pigheaded and haughty now, your father was merely headstrong then. And he'd decided that what he

wanted for his birthday was to explore the Coventry caves.

It was said that desperate people inhabited some of the caverns — witches and warlocks whose evil tempers, burning resentments, and self-centered fears had made them outcasts and exiles and driven them underground. Some were truly crazy, madmen.

Instead of being discouraged, Thantos claimed that running into such frightening creatures would add to the thrill.

Nathaniel felt it was too dangerous. "Felt," I suppose, is too weak a word. He sensed it, I think. He knew it. Yet I teased and goaded him into going. Not with his son, but with me.

We would inspect the caves, map the way, choose a safe route. And then, on Thantos's birthday, we would all go together.

Why? I have asked myself a thousand times. Why did I insist? Why did I so callously pressure my truest friend, laugh at his objections, and coax him to ruin?

The answers are never reassuring. I missed our old friendship, Nate's and mine. Selfishly, I wanted him to myself, wanted his attention and good company again. And here at last was a trek Leila would not accompany us on. More arrogant and foolhardy than I *ever was again, I agreed with a green boy, a willful child, that it would be an adventure. The rest of the story is known. I have not lived a day since then without regret.*

We weren't long into our underground journey when it happened. One of those frightening creatures, one so desperate he'd truly become a madman, ran at me carrying a spear of forged iron. Before I could defend myself, Nathan, true to our childhood vows, leaped in front of me.

I saw the deadly rod fly at his chest. Without thinking twice, I tackled Nate and knocked him down. Out of harm's way, I thought. Until the lunatic warlock began to laugh. He was slapping his knee and laughing and pointing at Nate.

I turned toward my friend and saw blood gushing from his head. He had hit the cave wall as he fell. He sat slumped, limp against the cold, wet stones. As the madman disappeared into the darkness, I rushed to Nathan, thinking I'd help him up, that I could stem the blood with herbs, bind his wound with strips of my own cloak, and carry him from the accursed cave.

He read my mind and sent back a terrible message. I will not leave alive.

And as I came nearer, I saw that my best friend was mortally wounded. The wall against which he

leaned was all that was keeping his shattered skull together. I wanted to protect him. Instead, I killed him.

As had been foretold, the curse claimed a new victim.

Because of an Antayus, the bravest and brightest DuBaer was murdered. Exactly as Abigail's son had decreed.

CHAPTER THIRTEEN
CRAILMORE

Crailmore, the DuBaer estate, was, as advertised, magnificent and scary. A soaring structure on the cliff crest of a cold and choppy sea, it seemed to preside over Coventry Island, or maybe lord over it. A welcoming shelter? Or foreboding fortress? It depended, Alex guessed, on which DuBaer was in residence and in command at the time.

As she trudged behind Ileana and Cam, who was keeping a deliberate distance from her sister, Alex's gray eyes swept over every detail of the impressive old house, noting the small touches: stained-glass windows aglow in the amber twilight, the weedy, still-fragrant remains of once lush flower beds, and smoke curling from fireplace chimneys.

Cam shuddered in the shadow of the looming house. The mansions of Marble Bay's wealthiest district also sat high above water, but they were lovingly landscaped and maintained. While Crailmore was larger and grander than any of them, its walls dripped with moisture, a briny sea mist that reminded Cam of sweat; and its stone facade and high fence made the place look like a prison. An effect that was sharpened when the iron gates creaked open automatically as the trio approached. The massive front door also swung back before they could ring the bell.

A servant, a light-haired young warlock, appeared immediately. He reminded Cam of Shane. She wondered whether, when he was in training with Thantos, Shane had also been one of her uncle's servants. And then she found herself wondering whether he was still . . .

"No," Alex's voice broke into Cam's thoughts. But she was talking to butler boy. "I'm Artemis. That's my sister, Apolla, but you can call us Cam and Alex," she was saying.

Surprised and embarrassed that a mainlander, even one of the fabled DuBaer twins, could so easily read his mind, the young warlock flushed. "I . . . thank you. I mean, I'm so sorry," he said, flustered. Then, clearing his throat, he declared, "Welcome to Crailmore. If you'll follow me, I'll show you to the sitting room where Lord Thantos is waiting."

Ileana, Cam, and Alex followed him down a broad, richly carpeted hallway. Marble pedestals holding antique vases, candelabras, and sculpted busts lined the corridor. Gilt-edged mirrors and gold-framed portraits hung on the walls.

Emily Barnes, Cam's interior decorator mom, would have busted the elaborate, meant-to-impress decor. "Garish, overdone, showy," was how she'd put it. Just thinking of Emily gave Cam a wretched twinge of homesickness. She suspected her twin was not feeling the same way — but would not ask, nor tap into Alex's head.

They weren't speaking.

They weren't even exchanging telepathic messages.

Cam was still wounded. And Alex had given up trying to explain why she'd decided to withhold the Shane info. If Cam insisted on feeling betrayed — whatever!

Ileana's head was reeling and her heart pounding. She was determined *not* to be impressed, not to feel anything here. Still, her awe and anger were uncontainable. This vast palace, with its glittering history and treasures on display, should have been hers. Instead, she'd been banished, abandoned on the far humbler doorstep of a warlock who had no interest in wealth, property, or prestige. Her rising rage was tempered only by a soul-deep truth: She'd been better off growing up with Karsh, saved, probably.

But her senses were in disarray: gratitude battling resentment, wonder tempering fear. The twins' contradictory thoughts, which kept intruding on her own, only added to Ileana's chaos.

She turned to look back at Alex and almost crashed into Cam. The girl had stopped suddenly and now stood staring at one of the largest gilt-framed paintings. In it a handsome young man with thick, dark hair and smiling eyes was portrayed in an old-fashioned pose. He held a soothsaying globe — a crystal ball — in one hand and with the other clasped a leather-bound book to his chest. Over the fingers clutching the book was draped a delicate chain from which a round amulet dangled. The coin-shaped charm was inscribed with a dancing bear wearing a crown.

"The DuBaer family crest," Ileana said aloud. "That's your grandfather, Nathaniel."

"He's your grandfather, too," Alex pointed out, stepping closer to the portrait and, incidentally, closer to Cam, who bristled at her nearness.

A tiny tremor, an electrical buzz, flashed between them. Under Nathaniel's smiling gaze, they both sensed

Cam's sudden craving to grasp her sister's hand and her stubborn unwillingness to give in to it.

Stepping away from Alex, she asked quickly, "Is it like our amulets?"

"You mean, does it have magical properties? Yes," Ileana responded as Alex, hiding her hurt and annoyance, continued along the gallery. "That's what amulets are: talismans, good-luck charms, to put it crudely. And I'd guess that particular one is very strong, since it carried not only 'our' grandfather's power but Lord Karsh's love, as well."

Cam glanced over at her twin to see whether she'd heard what Ileana said and to check out her sister's reaction to the info.

What she saw took her breath away.

Alex was bathed in light. Several feet away, a white brightness radiating from her, she stood staring up at another painting. She seemed lit up from the inside, Cam crazily thought, like the light-up plastic goose lamp Cam had as a child.

This time, even Ileana could feel the electricity that passed between them, Ileana, and the startled young servant — and the luminous woman who'd entered the hallway unnoticed.

"I see you've found your father," the woman said. It was her voice the twins recognized before her face and body.

Hands extended to take theirs, Miranda swept toward her children. But it was a new Miranda, wonderfully alive with clear gray eyes and skin shining, free of pallor and worry. She had released her golden-brown tresses from the confines of her braid, and her hair, so like Cam's — and Alex's true auburn — cascaded in waves of shimmering silk.

Her costume was of silk: she wore a fresh white tunic, a long, loose coat that fell to her ankles, and soft velvet slippers that, though they were white, reminded Ileana and her charges of Karsh's scuffed, black velvet shoes. Miranda took Cam's hand and put a slender arm over Alex's shoulder. With Ileana beside them, they studied the portrait Alex had discovered.

Ileana, of course, recognized Aron. Her throat thickened at once with tears, which, out of habit, she refused to shed. He looked exactly as she remembered him when she was fourteen and he was the handsome, gentle, fun-loving man she'd wished was her father. Aron's eyes, gray as her own, as Miranda's, and his true daughters', gazed down at her now as compassionate and loving as they had in life.

In the painting, he stood tall and lean against a vivid blue sky. His dark hair whipped by wind, his cape billowing. Behind him, at a distance, Crailmore rose on the cliffs.

Slowly, Cam realized her jaw hurt. Her mouth had been open since she'd seen her sister glowing weirdly, since Miranda, her stunningly rejuvenated birth mother, had entered the gallery, since she'd seen and "recognized" — there was no other way to put it — the father she'd never known.

Cam's lip trembled. Tears welled up. She would never know the man in the portrait. Her sorrow doubled, because now that she knew what he looked like, she knew she'd never again think of David Barnes as her daddy, no matter how hard she might try.

Slowly, Cam became aware of Miranda's hand in hers. And the strange warmth that embraced the three of them — her mother and sister and her. She wondered whether she, too, was glowing.

Most of all, she wondered what her father had said. This father, the handsome young warlock in the painting. Because he had said something to her the moment Miranda's hands had united them. Aron had whispered something. *I will be with you; I always have,* Alex told her sister. That's what he said. Miranda's eyes glistened with tears as she stared up at her lost husband. But her sadness, if that was what she was feeling, Ileana noticed, didn't diminish the remarkable change in her. She looked years younger, lighter, less timid, less dowdy.

With one of the only powers left to her, Miranda

heard Ileana's thoughts. She turned, stepping away from her girls, to Ileana. "It's being here," she confided. "Here where their spirits are most alive."

"They?" Ileana asked.

Miranda gestured to a painting on the opposite wall. It was of Leila and her children. The boys were very young, gathered around her: Fredo, small and sickly thin, clutching the skirt of her long gown; Thantos, beefy, grinning brashly, his arms crossed, stood in front of her; Aron was at her right, with Leila's hand resting lovingly on his shoulder.

"Aron and Leila," Miranda explained. "Their presence here in paintings, old photographs, and so many memories . . . I feel as though they're with me, protecting and guiding me." She lowered her voice modestly. "Blessing me."

"I know," Ileana replied. "I feel Karsh's love that way at his house and . . . well, everywhere on the island." She crossed the room and stood before Leila's portrait.

This woman who Miranda so treasured, Ileana's proud, imperious grandmother, had been responsible for uprooting Ileana, casting her out of this, her birthplace, her birthright — and for turning Thantos, that greedy, arrogant mama's boy, against his own wife and daughter. Because they were of Antayus blood. And because the old woman believed in the curse.

A sudden bitter wind distracted Ileana. She turned

toward its source, the doorway at the end of the gallery, which supposedly led to the sitting room. "Dolt, you leave me waiting?! How long does it take to bring my guests to me?" a booming voice raged.

And there he was. Her father, filling the door frame, glaring at the servant boy who now lay at his feet, frozen, literally frozen, into a grotesque ice sculpture.

Miranda and the twins saw the terrible scene, too, and gasped.

It was their shock and dismay, Ileana was sure, that caused her furious father to defrost the young warlock and pretend it had all been a joke.

As the boy scrambled away, Thantos came toward them. "Blessed?" he said, smiling at Miranda, "did I hear someone speak of being blessed? No more than I am, dear sister. Look at the beautiful brood that honors my home."

Cam shuddered and, despite the afternoon's upset, met Alex's hand halfway. Miranda looked stunned, her eyes still riveted to the puddle on the carpet where Thantos's fledgling had lain. With every ounce of contempt she could muster, Ileana met the foul tracker's gaze and returned his counterfeit grin. "Daddy," she cooed with almost tangible hatred.

Unshaken, Thantos took Miranda's arm and led her toward the door. "Come along," he called over his shoulder, "I mustn't ignore my other guests."

CHAPTER FOURTEEN
SEVEN FOR SUPPER

The sitting room was multiplex-sized and could comfortably contain a crowd. But only two chairs were occupied. Both faced a walk-in fireplace where flames hissed and crackled. Above the mantel, another portrait hung. This one was the most flamboyantly framed, indeed. It was the largest, most grandiose canvas of all.

In it, a bandy-legged, barrel-chested man with glittering black eyes and a beard as cropped and black as Thantos's glowered arrogantly. Wearing a black cloak, his trousers tucked into cuffed leather boots, he stood with one hand on his hip.

Thantos saw that the painting had, as intended,

commanded the newcomers' attention. "Do you know who that is?" he asked like a proud professor.

From one of the armchairs facing the fire, a breathless, whiny voice piped up. "I know, I know. It's Jacob DuBaer."

Alex instantly recognized the voice. As if to confirm it, her head ached suddenly where, a week ago, one of her uncle Fredo's violent sons had pulled her hair.

She glanced quickly at Cam and saw by her sister's horror-stricken expression that she also knew who had spoken.

"No fair, Tsuris," Thantos's other seated guest complained. "Uncle Thantos gave you the answer."

It was Vey, the chunky monkey who had assaulted Cam in Salem Woods . . . and then brought Karsh down. . . . Shaking with fury, Cam tried to control herself, to replace rage with reason. Shutting her eyes, she sensed Ileana stiffen beside her.

Instinctively, protectively, Cam took the alarmed witch's hand while Alex's fingers curled into fists as Karsh's killers stood leering gleefully. Alex erupted, "What are they doing here? They're murderers! How could you allow them to be here? They should be behind bars, in jail with their father!"

"Hey," said Tsuris, his twisted smile as cold as his ice-blue eyes.

"Yo, what's up?" the fireplug-shaped Vey giggled.

"I believe everyone is already acquainted," Thantos said, ignoring Alex, "except for Miranda."

Her smile suddenly frozen in place, Miranda stared at the odd couple, unnerved by their taunting, malicious tone.

"Miranda, meet your nephews, Tsuris and Vey, Fredo's sons. It occurred to me that our family reunion would be woefully incomplete without them."

Miranda wheeled to face Alex, understanding dawning on her. "They *killed* Karsh? Thantos said Lord Karsh's death was accidental."

Thantos raised his eyebrows in mock innocence. "It was. The poor boys inadvertently, purely by accident, totally unintentionally —"

"Murdered Karsh!" Ileana cut in.

"Oooo, she's still upset," Vey loudly confided to his brother.

"Well, wouldn't you be if you were, like, this big-deal witch who had a sudden power outage? Like, poof! No more magick?" Tsuris snorted.

"Gentlemen." Thantos stepped between his nephews and the women. "Please don't forget that tonight is a very special occasion. It is the first time that all living DuBaers, except for your father —"

"Who's in jail because of *her*." Vey glared at Ileana.

Thantos's smile wavered, his dark eyes flashed threateningly at Vey, who instantly — by choice or his uncle's dangerous will — fell back against his chair. "It's true that Ileana has not been the most devoted of DuBaers, but then again, she wasn't reared knowing her loyalties as you boys were," Thantos ventured charitably. "However, as my brother's widow has convinced me, it is time to welcome her home. She and Aron's children and you, Fredo's sons, are all that is left of our regal dynasty."

The servant boy returned with a tray of iced tea. Thantos took the first glass and, when everyone else was holding one, he lifted his to the bulky little man in the portrait. "To our heroic patriarch, Jacob DuBaer, the generous, good-hearted country doctor who saved dozens of witches and warlocks from persecution during the Salem Madness!"

All in the room politely raised their glasses, except for Ileana, who tossed hers into the fire, where it loudly shattered.

The others stared at her.

"I'll never drink to Jacob DuBaer," Ileana declared, "the jealous, lying wretch who hid his own warlock identity and sent Abigail Antayus, and who knows how many other good witches, to the gallows. Jacob DuBaer a hero? Ha! He was the dangerous madman who orphaned Abigail's children and instigated generations of needless bloodshed!"

In a final frantic gesture of disgust, Ileana snatched off the diamond earrings Thantos had given Beatrice and threw them at his feet.

Two people in the room knew what Ileana was ranting about.

Miranda understood a little. But this was not the moment, she decided, to get into it.

Thantos understood a little more. So, his reckless, arrogant daughter had unearthed a bit of DuBaer history. How? he wondered. It didn't matter. He'd have to disabuse her and her audience now — before she said too much.

A bell rang. Thantos's hapless servant cleared his throat. Still, his voice squeaked and quivered as he announced, "Dinner is served."

The fierce tracker took a deep breath and, with effort, found his hosting voice again and took Miranda's arm. "Let's eat, then," he said. Then, setting a foot down firmly on the precious stones, he turned his back on his audacious offspring and ground his wife's earrings into the cold, stone floor.

The dining room was a hub of hushed activity; serving people came and went, carrying baskets of bread, covered silver trays, and several platters simmering with delectable fare.

Grains and meats and greens of every description were deposited on a banquet table big enough to hold a massive floral arrangement and three very large candelabras.

Thantos clapped his hands and the flow of servants ebbed. Noiselessly, young witches and warlocks and a few elderly staffers set down their dishes and backed out of the room. Crailmore's guests circled the long table looking at the place cards that had been laid out — and which suited no one.

Miranda was seated opposite Thantos at the far end of the table; her nephews had been placed on either side of her, while her daughters were several feet away, flanking their uncle. Ileana sat midway down the long board, with Alex on her left and the treacherous Vey at her right.

Alex considered using her telekinetic skill to shuffle the place cards. But Miranda pleaded with her thoughts and eyes to leave things as they were. *For the sake of family harmony*, she proposed.

"There will be no disruptions at my table."

Thantos let it be known, like the Wizard of Oz, Cam thought — underwhelmed — that he knew, saw, and heard all. He was smiling again, back in his good-guy, great-leader mode.

Scramble the Oz image, Alex warned, guessing that four of the six other guests at the table would know exactly what Cam had T-mailed her twin. *This is so not a safe communication zone*.

Well, duh, Ileana sent back mischievously.

Cam and Miranda giggled. Thantos did not. And Tsuris and Vey glared around the table knowing they'd been left out, but not out of what.

Miranda, with her honed sense of fairness, sought to include them. "How is your mother?" she asked. "It's been a very long time since I saw her. You were just babies —"

"Vey was the baby," Tsuris sullenly accused. "I was hardly even born when Ahma moved back to California."

"Ahma?" Ileana said without thinking. "Isn't your mother's name Coco?"

Tsuris blushed furiously, but his thrust-forward jaw and evil squint made him look more menacing than embarrassed.

"He couldn't talk good when he was little," Vey gleefully explained. "He couldn't even say mama right. So he called her Ahma. How dumb is that, huh? Now we both do it."

"She doesn't like you, anyway," Tsuris told Miranda. "Ahma says all the DuBaers were either stuck-up or stupid. She thought you were stuck-up —"

"Yeah, and Papa was stupid," Vey added helpfully.

"How proud she must be that your father's genes are dominant in both of you nitwits," Alex said. To Cam she telegraphed, *It's raining idiots.*

"Huh? Gene who? What are you talking about?" Vey asked, perplexed.

"We'd tell you, but we don't speak Moron," Cam finished him off.

But Miranda gave her a small shake of the head. "Coco wasn't a witch," she explained to her daughters. "She found us . . . difficult to understand. I hope she's well," she said to Tsuris and Vey.

They shrugged in unison. "She didn't want us to come here," Vey muttered, "but Daddy did."

"You should always obey your mother," Cam dryly advised.

"Pops said he needed us," her cousin continued, "to, you know, get even."

"How DuBaer," Ileana murmured. "Vengefulness runs in our veins."

"It is not a trait exclusive to the DuBaers, Ileana," Thantos said, helping himself to a chop. "Your mother's

family, the Antayus clan, was infamous for exacting revenge."

A bit defensively, Miranda said, "Surely not all
Antayuses are dangerous?"

"Yeah, but *she* is," Tsuris whined again. "We were at
the trial. We saw."

"What of Lord Karsh?" Miranda proposed. "The gen-
tlest warlock to ever live."

"Who just happened to be murdered," Ileana
sneered, "by your honored guests."

"Chickens coming home to roost," Thantos snapped,
instantly seeing an opportunity to put his spin-control
plan into action. Whatever Ileana thought she knew
about their family history, he was about to change.

"I don't get it," Vey admitted.

"It's simple, really, and ironic and fitting," Thantos
went on. "Did you know that Karsh, the old tracker you
killed, was the very warlock who murdered your grandfather Nathan?"

Cam and Alex were bewildered but unable to get a
word in.

"It was an accident!" Ileana shouted, banging her
fist on the table, "Karsh was trying to *save* Nathaniel."

Thantos continued without acknowledging his
daughter. "Oh, yes. Diabolically clever was good Karsh.

First he befriended my father. Through wiles and witch-craft he convinced Nathaniel of his sincerity and friend-ship. But once my father was off guard, Karsh lured him down into the caves."

"It was *your* idea," Ileana contradicted. "You wanted to explore them."

Thantos shook his head as if he were truly sad-dened by Ileana's lunacy. Turning back to his other guests, he resumed. "It was well known that evildoers, maniacs, dwelled in the dark grottoes of the caves. And few knew that better than Ileana's devious guardian. Karsh himself had brought food and blankets and healing herbs to the demented scum who hid underground. So he knew what perils awaited my father there. But it was not a pitiful maniac who murdered Nathaniel DuBaer. It was the man who called himself my father's best friend."

"They *were* best friends." Ileana's voice rose dan-gerously. "Karsh loved Nathaniel and was loved by him in return —"

Thantos ignored her completely. "And when he emerged carrying my father's shattered body, the old trick-ster claimed that he had tried to save Nathaniel from the sword of a madman. But it was Karsh himself who crushed my father's skull. He was Antayus through and through, sworn to bring down the house of DuBaer."

"Lies and distortions!" Ileana could not contain herself and sprang up from the table.

"Of course your hotheaded guardian would say that." Thantos smiled benignly at his nieces. "Since she herself is Antayus . . . and sworn to do harm to our kind."

Shocked and dumbstruck, Cam and Alex had followed the exchange like spectators at a tennis match. Only they had no idea who had the advantage or even what game was really being played. There was some kind of ancient feud between Karsh's clan and their own?

Now both looked at Ileana. She was crimson; tears of frustration were gathering in her beautiful gray eyes.

Miranda was upset, though Alex intuited that her birth mother knew something of this.

Thantos said sorrowfully, "Alas," turning to his open-mouthed nephews, "you are the next generation of DuBaer sons."

"So?" Tsuris demanded.

"So Ileana's gonna try to kill us," Vey explained blithely. "Fat chance. Yo, bro, pass the salt," he ordered, stifling a laugh.

Snickering, his brother plucked up the heavy pewter saltshaker and hurled it across the table, missing Ileana's cheek by inches. The shocked witch ducked just in time.

"Aw, you missed," Vey grumbled.

"Boys, boys," Thantos scolded with fatherly indulgence.

"Boys?" Cam exclaimed angrily. "They're animals!"

"Amphibians?" Alex slyly suggested.

"Swamp meat," Cam agreed. "Do you remember how it goes?"

"The beginning, yeah," Alex said, holding her moon charm. "*Good magick that lights the night,*" she recited. "*Um, moon and stars that make the sky bright.*"

Clutching her sun amulet, Cam chimed in, "*Take this creature as we request; turn it into —*"

"How dare you!" Thantos thumped the table with his fist. Everyone jumped. But Vey jumped farthest of all. His webbed feet hit the floor with a sucking splat.

"Look what you did!" Tsuris shrilled, staring at his brother, who was Vey from the waist up, green and frog-legged below, and hopping frantically around the dining room.

"Now he looks like what he is: a half-brained half-toad. Let's finish," Alex said to Cam.

"You will do no such thing! Not while I'm the head of this family." Thantos pushed back his chair and stood abruptly, towering over them. "Is this what your guardian taught you?" he demanded, leaning forward, his face a picture of unmasked hatred. "To show off at my table, to shamelessly flex your fledgling magick in my face? Undo the spell at once. This is my house. Do you dare challenge me? I am the rightful head of this family. No girl child will ever unseat me. No matter what that murdering old warlock may have told you, I am the just heir to the DuBaer dynasty."

Now Miranda stood. "Stop it!" she shouted. Then, seemingly appalled at her outburst, she breathed deeply and moderated her voice. "Thantos, you have been kind to me all these years. And the kindest thing you have ever done is to reunite me with my daughters. I will be forever grateful to you. But now it is my place to discipline them . . . if I believe they need it."

"Undo the spell!" Thantos commanded, ignoring her.

Miranda sat back down, looking stunned and angry. Ileana hurried to her and laid an arm over her shoulder.

The twins turned toward their mother and their guardian, both of whom had less power over their uncle right now than they did.

Only if you want us to, Cam telegraphed the women.

For the sake of family harmony, Alex teased.

Their mother looked up at Ileana, grasping the younger witch's comforting hand. Ileana nodded her consent.

"Undo the spell," Miranda gently told her children.

CHAPTER FIFTEEN
THE TRAP

Cam and Alex spent a mostly sleepless night, their last on Coventry. In the afternoon, they'd journey back to the mainland. The night air, oppressively muggy, and the still strange sounds of the forest filtered in through the screen of Ileana's open bedroom window. But the twins' restlessness had little to do with humidity or creepy woodland noises.

Their stomachs were churning from dinner — the food and the fiasco. They'd learned too much about their regal family. And not nearly enough.

Now Alex wasn't sure she wanted to leave. She didn't feel ready. Oh, her bag was packed — compliments of compulsive Cam — and they had return reservations on the three P.M. ferry, but . . .

Alex thought suddenly of Evan, her Montana homey, going, "Yo, Als, don't sweat it. It's natural you want to stay. These are your peeps, dude. This is your 'hood." The idea made her laugh aloud, rankling Cam, who kicked her in the darkness.

So why was she sweating it?

Miranda, Ileana, even the psycho uncle and retard cousins — for better or worse, they were her peeps. Her blood.

Coventry was her birthplace, the final resting place of her father, her grandparents, and beloved Karsh. One day, it might be hers, too. Although she'd been taken from here when she was barely a day old, reared until she was fourteen in Crow Creek, Montana, and then been welcomed into Cam's family in Marble Bay, Massachusetts, this strange little island was her 'hood.

Exiting it now would be like leaving a really cool jigsaw puzzle unfinished. In this short, sad visit, an important picture had begun to form, but Alex couldn't make out the details yet. Her personal list of missing pieces, or "stuff she didn't get," was topped by last night's bizarre revelation.

There was some weird clan war going on. Thantos,

Ileana, and even Miranda were in on this family secret — but disagreed violently on the details. She and Cam had not been looped in on any of this, not even by Karsh. Worst was Thantos's words ringing in her ears: "Ileana herself is Antayus . . . and sworn to do harm to our kind."

What was *that* about? No way would Ileana ever hurt them. She might cast a vengeful spell on Tsuris and Vey, but hey — they started it! They'd tried to kill *her*! And Thantos, Ileana's own father, had been egging the fried-brain boys on. You didn't need Cam's super-sight to see the hulking unc for what he was: rotten to the core.

But what was Shane's agenda? And The Furies, who fascinated and repelled her. Alex needed to understand them, so she could know how to fight them.

She flipped over and buried her head in the pillow.

There is time still. By morning's light, roam the island. Alone. Then understanding will come to you and only you, Artemis.

Alex's eyes flew open. She rolled over, inducing a monster sigh of annoyance from Cam. For a split second, she was back in the trailer in Montana. This time, the voice she heard wasn't Evan's. Nor was it Karsh's. This voice was female. But whose? Ileana's? Miranda's?

She blinked. *By morning's light* . . . The ferry wasn't coming for several hours. Someone capable of breaking into her head had urged her to keep searching. By herself.

Soon after dawn, alone, Alex headed into the woods.

Cam was annoyed. Wired, edgy, irritated. More so because she shouldn't have been. The safety and comfort of Marble Bay, of Dave, Emily, her brother, Dylan, her friends, was less than twenty-four hours away. Once home, she could let all this, Coventry, its colorful characters and creepy warnings, fade into the background, where — for now, anyway — it belonged. She was only fifteen, she reminded herself. Didn't she deserve a few more "normal" years before having to deal?

Still, something gnawed at her. Maybe it was the word "deserve." Had Alex "deserved" to grow up in poverty. Had Aron "deserved" to die the day his daughters were born, Miranda to go mad with grief?

You don't get what you deserve, not always. "You get what you get," Cam's friend Sukari said. Now Cam knew what she meant.

If only she could "will" a vision to come to her. Be proactive instead of reactive. Do something instead of just waiting . . . for the ferry . . . for Alex . . . for a clue to what was coming next. When she was younger, her intuition, her premonitions had been simpler. A car speeding around a corner? Get Beth out of the way. A deserted road, an old garage? That's where the kidnap victim was being held.

But here, on Coventry? Her premonitions were of wounded, bellowing animals, terrified and faraway, needing her. And the fabulous floating-eyes vision. Another creature. But she didn't know where or what it was or how she could help it.

Cam's jitters were even worse this morning. Alex had bounced, gone off to explore. Which left Cam and her annoyingly unfocused irritation alone. Like an itch she couldn't pinpoint, Cam didn't know where to scratch.

A chick chat would be *so* welcome right now.

Only . . . phone? No service.

IM-ability? Neither laptop, nor Palm, nor text-messaging PDA in sight.

And hours to go before the Bumpster pulled his boat into Coventry harbor. Do something, her nerves urged. Keep moving! Time will go faster, the nagging thingie, the eerie feeling that trouble is on the way again, might fade. Cam looked around. Alex had cleaned the mess made by Tsuris and Vey. But surely there was more to do.

With edgy energy to burn, she started in the kitchen. But while she switched the bowls with the goblets, stacked the ceramic mortar and pestles like so much

Tupperware, alphabetized the herbs and spices, she still could not dodge the icky foreboding. The dread.

Cam willed herself to think about *her* peeps. "Just talk, Cam, I'll listen," is what Beth would say, big round brown eyes full of real empathy.

"A problem shared is a problem halved," Amanda would coo. "You're only as sick as your secrets."

"Oh, just deal, Barnes!" Brianna would interrupt snippily with an impatient wave of her hand.

Bree won.

Deal. Okay, Cam would deal. She'd figure out what was tugging at her, rooting her here — just when it was time to go back.

Shane? No. Not Shane. Maybe Shane.

Okay, she was conflicted. For a moment, she'd agreed with Alex's decree of "can't be trusted." Then she'd seen him again. And melted. "Get real!" she told herself, moving into the sitting room and shifting the velvet hassock from the foot of the easy chair to just in front of the fireplace. The boy was all Etch-a-Sketch-y: Draw whatever picture, tell whatever story he wanted, and if it didn't work, shake up the game and try again. He told her what was convenient, not what was true. Yesterday, out back by the hammock, she'd asked him where exactly he lived. Where had his non-girlfriend Sersee found him a place?

He'd dodged her question, gone cliché. "Nothing to write home about. It's small, damp, claustrophobic. Not a lot of light."

Cam flashed on a vampire's lair. He laughed, reading her mind. "Home sweet home isn't quite so voodooish as that."

"Besides," he veered toward a three-cliché pileup, "it's just a place to hang my cape. It's not really . . . home."

Some people had two homes, she thought.

Shane had read her mind. His hands gently framing her face, his intense eyes riveting her, he argued, "No. Only *one* real one. Yours is here, Apolla. Maybe not today or next week or even next year, but one day, you'll know . . . here." He placed her hand over his heart. "Which is the only place that counts."

He'd left her that afternoon with a soft sweet kiss and a promise to see her again. So did Sersee have real reason to be jealous? Or was the jealousy hers? Of Sersee. Is that why she sorta wanted to stay?

She'd begun to rearrange the photos on the mantel when her sense of dread spiraled upward. She stopped, holding a picture in midair. Someone was approaching, and it was neither Alex nor Ileana. A male.

Shane again? No. Not his gait. Then Thantos? Tsuris? Vey? In readiness, Cam focused her fiery eyes set to fry an unwelcome intruder.

Unwelcome?

Try unbelievable. This could so not be happening — not again! Her two worlds collided, so did her emotions. Relief that he seemed okay crashed head-on into terror. He was there at her front door this time.

"Jason?" she asked haltingly.

Several days of stubble covered his chin; his cheeks were gaunt, concave almost, his shirt was ripped and filthy. Still, a wistful smile played on his lips. His eyes, dark, intense, were not similar to the eyes she'd seen in her dream and in her premonition. They were identical.

"I need you to come with me." That was all he said. No explanation, no greeting. Not like Jason at all.

Struggling to keep it together, Cam stammered, "You . . . you . . . shouldn't be here. I sent you back . . . the ferry . . ." She tried to pinpoint what was wrong — besides everything.

When Jason was bugged, he squirmed, shoving his hands in his pockets. When he was nervous, he covered it up with a joke. He was totally serious now.

In a smooth, soothing, almost trancelike voice, he said again, "You need to come with me, honey."

Honey? Where'd Cheese-boy come from?

"Jason," Cam started again, hoping she sounded calm and rational, "I can't come with you until I know why you're here. Why you didn't go back."

Robotically, he responded, "I'm here to help you."

"But, remember, I told you." Cam's voice rose, approaching alarm. "I didn't need any —" She paused and took a deep breath. "Come in," she managed. "We need to talk."

Instead, Jason moved closer and put his arm around her shoulder. "Come with me. We can talk on the way, my little witch."

Goose bumps raised on her arms. Who was this imposter? If not a clone, maybe a warlock morphed into Jason? She scanned his face carefully. The little vein pulsing in his forehead? Yes. Lucky b-ball charm around his neck? Check. Although he'd obviously lost weight, it was Jason all right. Only not.

If she didn't go with him, she'd never know what was going on.

If she did, he could be leading her — well, who knew where?

She sent a telepathic shout-out to Alex, then closed the door behind her and followed him into the woods. "Jase," she tried again as they walked deeper into the forest, "why didn't you leave? Or tell me you were still here? Where've you been for the past two days?"

"Right under your nose, honey-bunny."

Honey-bunny . . . My little witch? Cam zoomed from panicked to seriously ticked off. She grabbed his elbow hard, and even though he was a head taller, swung him around. "What's going down? Who are you? Where are you taking me?"

His mouth opened as if to form the answer.

But Cam didn't hear him. Her head buzzed, her eyes blurred. A vision flashed before her. He was taking her to LunaSoleil.

Alarmed, she whizzed another telepathic SOS to her twin. And sent two more — to Miranda and Ileana. She needed help. Now would be a good time.

When they got to Aron and Miranda's house, Jason led her straight around the back and brushed away the camo pile of twigs, leaves, and dirt covering the cellar door. As he guided her down the dark stairs, he clasped his hands around her waist protectively so she wouldn't slip. Or run away.

At the bottom, Jason steered her in a U-turn behind the steps. It was the only part of the basement she hadn't thought to examine. Big mistake. She'd have scoped out the trapdoor. The squeaking floorboards would have spoken volumes to Alex.

Realization hit hard. Sersee was behind all this.

Half credit. The leader of the sorceress sorority was actually *under* all this.

In the caves.

The trapdoor led down a set of slippery stone

steps, which ended at the foot of a winding, sloping tunnel. "Go," Jason said tonelessly, his hands on her shoulders now, urging her forward. He seemed to not hear her questions, her protests. The farther in and down they went, the darker, danker, creepier it got. Not unlike Shane's description of where he lived.

Finally, some distance away, a dim light appeared. It wasn't sunlight. As she got closer, Cam saw hanging lanterns, sconces, and candles.

The caves of Coventry Island, Cam remembered Shane's history lesson. Once a haven for persecuted witches, more recently training grounds for Thantos's apprentices. As she'd heard last night, a place where spirits, outcasts, maniacs dwelled still. Where her grandfather had been killed.

"Like grandfather, like granddaughter." Sersee appeared, clothed in black from hood to cloak to boots. "Apolla. Welcome to our . . . let's see, what would a mainlander say? Oh, that's right. Our *crib*. Welcome to our crib. Do make yourself comfortable. You'll be staying for some time. In fact, does forever work for you?"

CHAPTER SIXTEEN
THE DESTINY

Ileana awoke with a start from a terrifying dream.

Something was rustling through her garden, tramping down her herbs. It was a child. No, it was *half* a child, a little girl missing half her face and body as if a sword had sliced her in two . . .

One of the twins, Ileana thought. *Was it Cam? Or Alex?*

Eyes stubbornly shut, the wakeful witch shuddered and shifted, trying to get comfortable in Karsh's bed, which felt even narrower than usual this morning.

This half-being, one of two identical parts, was walking behind a dark, dangerous animal. Though she was following the creature, Ileana knew that the girl was destined to lead . . .

There would be no more sleep, she realized miserably, tossing in the cramped, lumpy bed. She was awake. As the last wisps of the dream floated out of reach, Ileana cautiously and reluctantly opened her eyes.

That explained it. Some of it. She had fallen asleep in Karsh's decrepit old easy chair. She had never even gone to bed. Stretching stiffly — every bone in her beautiful body aching — she eased herself back to consciousness.

She had fallen asleep reading after returning from dinner at Crailmore — a family dinner with relatives who made the Manson family look like the Brady Bunch. Dysfunctional? More like Diss-functional. Insults and attitudes for the first course, attempted assault for dessert.

Ileana stood up and stubbed her bare toes on what felt like a brick but was only a book. A "book-alike" really, she thought, hopping on one foot so that she could massage the mashed toes of the other. Although its title read *Forgiveness or Vengeance,* it was little more than a leather-bound binder that held Karsh's urgent letter to her.

Now she remembered. She had come home last night furious, her head abuzz with questions, the taste of bile bitter in her throat. How dare he? she'd thought.

How dare that hulking egomaniac control freak, the disgusting DNA donor who was her father in genetics only, have defended Tsuris and Vey? How dare he compare those deadly dolts to gentle, good, and giving Karsh? And Thantos's version of the DuBaer family history? Lies, lies, lies.

Ileana gasped, remembering . . . remembering what she had read last night! She swept up Karsh's book and hobbled with it out to his garden. Already, the little plot was ravaged by weeds, its thirsty plants wilting, heads bowed like herbs in mourning.

Later, she'd work in the garden, Ileana promised herself. Now she wanted to review the stunning revelation of last night's reading. She turned quickly to the passage she'd read before the family fiasco. It had ended with Karsh's painful confession:

I wanted to protect him; instead I killed him.

As had been foretold, the curse claimed a new victim.

Because of an Antayus, the bravest and brightest DuBaer was murdered. Exactly as Abigail's son had decreed.

Ileana skimmed the page and found the remarkable passage she'd read last night:

Again, he read my thoughts, your grandfather, Nathaniel. No, you may not stay with me, dear friend.

You must go on living. Do not grieve, Karsh, *he silently ordered.* But carry out our plan. So that the Antayus curse may die with me. Change the order of succession. Tell my sons that none of them will rule, none lead. I am the last patriarch. But they will provide leaders — their wives and daughters.

From this day forward, only women will decide the fate of the DuBaer dynasty. Remarkable women, dedicated to good, to compassion and justice, schooled in the ways of our craft, Karsh had written, *and free, dear child, of the Antayus taint.*

Ileana looked up. So many things fell into place: Thantos's unbridled greed, his determination to head the family and control the wealth, had been more important than his dying father's wish. Of course he wanted Miranda and Ileana out of the way, and the twins, with their extraordinary powers. He would force them to accept and serve his authority. Or see them dead.

Thantos balked at his father's demand, denied that Nathaniel would have suggested such a thing, and spent most of his early years trying to cast doubt on the truth of my word. One of the ways he did this was to claim that his father's death had not been accidental and to spread it about that I had deliberately murdered Nathaniel.

But Leila and Rhianna knew better. They had

heard us speaking of our plan to put an end to the curse, knew that it was Nathaniel's desire, his desperate will, that Leila lead the family at his death. It was she who defended me against the vicious accusations of her own son. Your grandmother, along with tender Rhianna, tried to comfort me — even as she herself suffered the loss of her beloved husband.

Do not fear and do not falter, my fierce goddess. Do not let hatred weaken you. It is not seemly or serious. It is a joke one plays on oneself. For to hate, Ileana, is to drink poison and expect someone else to die. Cleanse your spirit, dear child of my heart, practice your craft, ask for help when you need it, and teach your fledglings by word and deed the power of good witches. There is so much yet to tell.

Karsh must have grown tired here. His hand faltered. His handwriting grew harder to read. And finally, the journal ended unfinished with the words, *It is up to you now, Ileana — to guide your charges to their destiny.*

So many things were left unexplained.

What destiny did he mean?

What did Karsh want the twins to do? Head the DuBaer clan? Thantos, wild with power and greed, would never allow it. And strong as they were, they were no match for him.

So perhaps he meant they should avenge his death by finishing off Tsuris and Vey, the only DuBaer males of their generation?

Or . . . did he mean for them to save their murderous cousins from death? Would that reverse the curse and thereby end it?

Alexandra and Camryn, Ileana knew well, could do neither. The twins could not kill, but just the same, they would not save the pair who'd killed their beloved Karsh. He would be in many ways the most important man in their lives. He'd made them whole by bringing them together. He'd sacrificed himself so they might live.

Leave it to Karsh, Ileana thought, fighting back tears. Leave it to the old trickster to bequeath her a monstrous riddle to unravel and to trust absolutely that she was capable of solving it.

CHAPTER SEVENTEEN
BETRAYED

Alex was on a quest. Guided by the message in her dream, warmed by Miranda's quilt, she roamed the island waiting for the jigsaw puzzle pieces to come together. Then she'd know what she had to do and when she'd have to do it.

She wandered randomly — Alex in Wonderland, she thought — absorbing the vivid colors and vibrant fragrances of the woods. Passing through a barrier of thick vines and bramble, she found herself at the water's edge. Today, the great lake mirrored the calm sky, sparkling with morning sunshine.

Coventry was not so far from the mainland, even if it seemed to exist in its own universe, floating without anchor. Alex knelt to examine the shells and pebbles delivered to shore by gentle waves. When a shimmering pink stone washed up, she examined it closely, turning it between her forefinger and thumb. It seemed to heat up in her hand. Or maybe she was flushed with feelings. It was a crystal of rose quartz. Karsh had given her one just like it.

Tenderly brushing sand from the multifaceted stone, she tucked it into her pocket and climbed aimlessly up a tall dune hairy with sea grass. At the top of the sandy hill, hidden by the grass, was a large boulder. Alex climbed it and looked down at the island. From this peak she could see practically everything, from the gleaming glass of the Unity Dome all the way to the cliffs of Crailmore.

She scrambled down the far side of the boulder and followed a rough, forested path to the village. There, she was struck again by the brilliant hues of houses, shops, and flowers cascading from baskets hung on every spiraled street lamp. The cobblestone avenues and sunny square, now at midmorning, began to fill with people in colorful capes, robes, or casual mainland clothing. They frequented spice, mineral, and herb shops, candle-making galleries and pottery barns, and breakfasted at the outdoor cafés around the village square. Every time Alex turned a corner, she felt as if she'd turned a page in a fairy tale picture book.

By the time she reached the far side of town, she knew without consciously thinking about it where her search would lead.

She arrived at LunaSoleil just before noon. The leaves and twigs hiding the cellar door had been brushed aside. Had she and Cam left it like that? There were two sets of footprints on the dusty steps leading down to the basement. Without Cam's super-vision, Alex couldn't tell if they were new or left over from her first visit. She stood completely still and listened hard.

Silence.

Reassured, Alex took the stairs two at a time and made for the loft. *Understanding will come to you, Artemis,* she'd been promised. Would she find it here in Aron and Miranda's peaceful space?

Everything she'd heard at dinner, about a curse, about family secrets, had rocked her. As if something had gently turned her head, her gaze fell on the cedar chest. Were there missing puzzle pieces inside? Would unlocking the old trunk also unlock old secrets?

The fragrant aromas of the herbs sprinkled on the linens filled her nostrils. Fishing beneath the soft pile, she pulled her father's hammer out of the trunk. She could picture his strong hand wrapped around it, his face lined in concentration as he shaped their amulets. Automatically, she reached for her moon charm and pictured Cam's sun.

Cam. The thought of her sister jolted her. Was Cam here? She stopped, listened, and heard nothing.

She found the strands of gold chain rolled up like a ball of yarn. Her dad had probably planned to lengthen their necklaces as they got older. How cruelly ironic that a man as gifted and powerful as Aron DuBaer had not known he wouldn't live to see his daughters grow up. She pocketed the remaining chain. It had been meant for her and Cam, and so it would be theirs.

Out of the corner of her eye, Alex caught something glowing and pushed everything away to uncover the source of the amber light. It was coming from the inside pocket of a lush burgundy velvet cape. Her curiosity on high-beam, she reached inside. Like the crystal she'd found, the small jewelry box began to radiate warmth.

Anxiously but gently, she opened it and recognized at once the large, coin-shaped amulet she'd seen in one of the portraits at Crailmore. She traced the dancing bear with her finger. The DuBaer family crest, she remembered, the one their grandfather, Nathaniel DuBaer, had been holding. He must have given it to Aron.

Now that she'd found it, she could return it to Miranda. Or, even better, she'd give it to Ileana. Her first DuBaer family talisman.

Alex snapped to attention, her keen hearing drawn to a noise outside. Footsteps? Someone was coming . . .

someone was . . . skipping? . . . closer to the house. How cool would it be if it were Cam?

Only, Cam walked purposefully, or she ran like the wind. She did not skip. Nor would she make that swishing sound, like a long cape brushing against old and brittle fallen leaves. And that . . . what? . . . soft singing? Camryn-the-unmusical? Nuh-uh.

Alex stuffed the DuBaer family crest into her back pocket alongside the gold chain. Someone was skipping around to the back of the house. Grasping Aron's hammer, she hurried back down to the cellar and, staring up at the double doors, she waited.

Noisily, the old doors flapped open. A figure silhouetted by the glare of the midday sun was about to descend the basement steps.

Shane? No, the crasher was female. Ileana? Too perky. Miranda? Too small.

Michaelina? The pixie witch hadn't even made the short list.

Alex gasped so loudly the littlest Fury lost her footing and tripped on the hem of her too-long cape. Yelping in shock, Mini-Mike bounced down the hard wooden steps on her butt. Shock turned to alarm when she saw Alex. "What are you doing here?"

"Right back atcha," Alex barked.

Michaelina's mind was racing. *She's here! What*

does she know? Did she go to the caves? Has she seen . . . ? Sersee didn't expect this —

"She didn't?" Sick at the idea of the vicious skeletor trespassing in her parents' home, Alex grabbed the frantic girl's hand and yanked her up roughly to keep her off balance — before Michaelina could scramble her thoughts. "Let's just see how your fearless leader deals with the unexpected."

Michaelina tried to pull away. Her struggle revealed a barbed-wire tattoo circling her scrawny biceps, a matching bracelet for her neck-tat. "That pass for cutting-edge cool in Fury Land?" Alex taunted, tightening her grip.

Through gritted teeth, Michaelina exclaimed, "Let go! Or else!"

"Or else what?" Annoyed as she was, Alex almost laughed. "You'll put a spell on me? Turn me into a frog? I don't think so."

Michaelina hung tough. "I could do some damage."

"But you won't," Alex declared. "Not until you give it up, girl. Chill and spill. Dish the dirt, get down and fess up, unburden your soul — whatever the locals say."

"I don't know what you're talking about," the thwarted witch growled.

"Yeah, you do. And you'll tell all. Don't mess with me, Michaelina. There's magick in this house. And it's all

176

advantage Alex." Where had that come from? Alex had no clue. It had tumbled out of her mouth, totally bypassing her brain.

Whatever. It worked. Sort of. Michaelina stopped struggling to free her hand. "Can I sit down — somewhere soft?" she asked plaintively.

Suddenly, Alex had released the girl and found herself undoing the fragile, herb-filled baby quilt she'd tied around her neck. A familiar scent wafted from it. Not a confused potpourri of fragrances, but the spicy odor of a single distinct herb. "Here, sit on this," Alex was about to offer, not knowing why. And then she snatched the quilt away and remembered: A spicy herb. A rose quartz crystal. An incantation. The truth inducer.

"What's that smell?" Michaelina was rubbing her wrist. "Rosemary, marjoram? Nothing has ever grown down here but mushrooms. And I've cleaned them all. Can I go now?"

"So you've been here before?" Alex asked, fishing the crystal from her pocket.

"Everyone on the island's been here at one time or another," Mike said casually, but her thoughts were scrabbling like mice looking for cheese.

"Ever seen one of these?" Alex tossed her the crystal. Michaelina automatically reached out and caught it.

"Rose quartz. How unique. Not." The little witch

pretended boredom, but Alex could see the crystal glowing and knew Mike was feeling the heat.

Which Alex was about to turn up.

She held the quilt under Michaelina's nose.

"Excuse me?" The feisty Fury made a sour face and pulled back her head. "What's that, your laundry?"

"No, I was . . . you know that spicy odor you smelled? I was hoping you could help me identify it."

"Do I look like a gardener? I'm a witch, Al-pal, not a landscaping expert." Still, she sniffed cautiously at the baby blanket. Her brow furrowed for a moment. Then she bent forward and sniffed again. And her face relaxed. She blinked for a bit, then asked sleepily this time, "Can I go?"

"One more question," Alex said. "There's this spell . . . I know most of it but I'm not sure of the ending —"

"Typical MAD: Mainland Attention Deficit," Michaelina said. Alex could see warring expressions struggling across the woozy witch's face. The Fury had tried to sneer but wound up smiling. "Don't tell anyone, but I'm Sersee's unofficial spell-check. That girl's head is thicker than her curls." Michaelina gasped, shocked by her own words. Then the silly grin returned and she shrugged. "Lay it on me," she urged Alex.

"Okay." Clutching her moon charm with one hand and, with the other, cupping Michaelina's hands, which still held the warm crystal, Alex began: *"Oh, moon that gives us light and cheer, shine through me now —"*

"No, no, no. No way," Michaelina interrupted. As Alex stiffened, the groggy witch said, "It's sun. Oh, *sun* that gives us light and cheer —"

Alex sighed with relief. "Right. *Oh, sun,*" she said, resuming the spell. *"Shine through me now to banish fear. Free Michaelina from doubt and blame —"*

"Free who? Me?"

"Let me win her trust," Alex hurried on, *"and lift her shame."*

Michaelina's lids began to flutter. "I thought," she murmured, struggling to keep her eyes open, "you wanted my help."

"Totally," Alex affirmed. "I don't just want it, I need it . . . desperately." Though the girl had gone slack, her tension drained away. The young witch was a hard case. What she said stunned Alex.

"You what?" she repeated, "You *live* here?"

"Not here," Michaelina mumbled, nodding in the direction of the cellar, "down . . . you know, there."

A sickening wave washed over Alex. Down there. The caves. Like The Furies of legend, she lived underground with — duh-uh — her fellow cellar-dwellers Sersee and Epic. Self-proclaimed outcasts, who believed they were "unstoppable."

"I know you helped us undo the spell Sersee used to transform the frog. Why did you betray her?" Alex prodded.

Michaelina, her hands in her lap, scoffed, "I didn't betray her. I just messed with her."

"Because she gets too big for her witchy-britches sometimes?" Alex guessed.

Michaelina narrowed her emerald eyes and lifted her delicate chin defiantly. "She thinks she knows everything."

"But she doesn't know you gave the spell to us, does she? She still thinks Cam and I figured it out by ourselves."

Michaelina shrugged. "That's what she thinks."

"What do The Furies want?"

"To rule," the thin witch recited mechanically. "We're younger, brighter, and stronger than the soft, old fools of the Unity Council who have forgotten what real witches can be. We want to go back to the old ways, when we were pure and powerful. We don't believe we're meant to serve the weak and needy. Sersee says it's the other way around."

"Right," Alex said, brushing the power-trip pep talk aside. "And where does Shane fit in?" She couldn't picture him "serving" Sersee. He wasn't exactly the basic obedient-follower type. The rebellious hunk had even disobeyed

Thantos when the mighty tracker had ordered him to kill.

"She needs him." Even in her trance state, Michaelina could pick brain with the best of them. "Sersee needs him. I mean, a lot of people, young people, are dazzled by her. They think she's smart and all powerful. Not even close. But Shane is. He's brilliant, gifted, and chosen — everything she's not. And he's this incredible teacher. He's taught her spells and stuff she'd never get on her own. Before you guys showed up, Shane was supposed to be the power behind Sersee's throne."

It clicked. Shane was the source of Sersee's craft-cleverness. And it didn't hurt that he was a graduate of the Thantos School of Underhanded Hotties. No way could the sly, violet-eyed temptress afford to lose him. "She's jealous of Cam," Alex said.

"Insanely, you could even say."

"That's why she hates us — all over a boy?" This was a concept Alex could never wrap her brain around.

"Not entirely," Michaelina confirmed. "It's about greed, too. You power princesses, that's what she calls you," Michaelina giggled, "stand to inherit a lot. DuBaer Industries, your parents' talents. You could rule this island."

"And Sersee couldn't stand to see that happen." Neither, it struck Alex, could Thantos.

"Can't stand to see it?" Michaelina echoed. "She won't let it happen. Together, you and sister sweetie-pie are more powerful than Sersee could ever hope to be. Her only chance is to separate you."

Separate us?

Realization struck like a thunderbolt. It hit Alex so hard she almost keeled over, clutching her stomach. Now, *right now* they *were* separated. The voice that had instructed her to roam the island — *alone!* Oh, no. It hadn't been Ileana or Miranda; it had been Sersee, sabotaging and separating them.

But why had she fallen for it? She knew the answer before putting the punctuation on — *because she was vulnerable*. Because she wanted to stay, to find answers. She followed it because it was telling her what she wanted to do, anyway. Her own desires had made her vulnerable. Just like now.

As if to confirm her insight, Alex began to feel dizzy. Holding onto the railing of the cellar stairs, she started to shake. And then the whooshing in her ears quieted and she heard a voice, muffled, terrified, but as recognizable as her own. Grabbing Michaelina's narrow shoulders, she demanded, "What have you done to my sister?"

CHAPTER EIGHTEEN
THE CAVES

She'd been ambushed.

Jason had been the bait. He hadn't left Coventry after all. Instead, he'd been lured back, used to lead Cam smack into a trap.

She had not seen it coming. She should have. Jason's glazed eyes, the bizarro things he was saying? Hello! Witchcraft 101, anyone? The boy was under a spell, cast by the cold, cruel toad-tormenter herself. At Sersee's say-so, he'd come to capture Cam.

Mission accomplished. She was deep in the heart of Sersee-land.

Epie tied Cam's hands behind her back and pushed her down onto a benchlike rock formation. She was a prisoner. But she would *not* go to pity-city right now. She would deal.

Calmly, Cam took stock of her situation. *Then* she went to pity-city.

She was alone and outnumbered. This was not the training ground Shane had told her about. It was Sersee's lair, in a section of the caves that had probably gone unexplored for decades — beneath LunaSoleil.

"Who said you were the slow one?" Sersee taunted her. "So far, you've aced it. Not many even know this part of the caves exists. Except for certain members of your own family. What sweet irony that you're here. Princess Apolla, meant to live in luxury above us, literally. Poor little sun queen, all in the dark now. The only DuBaer for miles around — and deep underground."

Resolutely, Cam refused to be baited. She would figure a way out of this. Taking a deep breath, she shoved all the how's and why's out of her head and concentrated on the what now. She'd have to fight for herself — and for Jason. Like an innocent bystander in a drive-by, he'd been caught in the cross-fire. He was standing zombie-like now in the shadows behind Sersee, waiting, Cam suspected, for his next instructions.

"So true, so true," the tall witch mocked her, reading her mind. "The disadvantages just keep piling up, don't they? Okay, I'll do one: Your telepathic powers, pitiful to start with, are all 'No Service,' down here."

With Sersee intercepting her thoughts, Cam forced herself not to think about her game plan — and then invent one. Only one idea, one word, escaped — *Soccer*.

"Sock me?" Sersee laughed. "With what? Your hands are tied."

Curlylocks hadn't gotten it. She didn't have a clue that Cam was ace forward for Marble Bay High's first-rate soccer team and that she could think, run, and score like a champ. To Cam, the single thought, Soccer, meant pulling a mental fake-out. Think one thing and do another. It was worth a try.

She concentrated on looking around and looking desperate, as if she were scoping out the cave, scanning for escape routes.

She watched Sersee watching her. Good.

Without warning, Cam leaped up and made a run for it. Faking to the left, then dashing to the right, she grabbed Jason's clammy hand and raced toward the tunnel.

But Jason was dead weight. Dragging him gave slick Sersee and lumpy Epie all the time they needed to make a Cam sandwich. Block complete. Game over.

"That's the best you can do?" Sersee sniped. "Run

away? Your ancestors would be appalled. You," she told Jason, pointing to where he'd been standing before. "Over there, pussycat."

Okay, *now* Cam felt panic rising. She squashed it. A freak-out or misstep like the one she'd just attempted and she'd be landfill. She'd have to outwit — or out-witch — her enemies, who knew every inch of this cave and island.

Epie pushed her down again and, this time, Cam studied her surroundings more closely.

Sersee, Epie, and Michaelina had staked out this cold, dank turf as their own. Tools of the trade were laid out on a natural stone shelf at the far end of the cavern: mortar and pestles to grind herbs and spices, to make potions and cast spells. But where were the herbs themselves, and the crystals? Clearly, stashed away so that no visitor or captive could use them.

There were crevasses in the cave walls, archways that led into separate spaces, dark igloos furnished with sleeping bags and oil lamps. There were four such "rooms." Four for three witches. With a sickening feeling, Cam realized this was the damp, dark place Shane had described as his home. He lived here. Where was he now? Lurking in his lair, waiting for Sersee's orders?

And were there still demented outcasts — present company aside — living in the underground passageways? Or spirits of the dead? She almost wished there were. They might divert Sersee's attention.

Which was again riveted on Cam. Without shifting her eyes, the glowering witch snapped her fingers at Epie. "Take her amulet," she commanded. "She won't be needing it anymore."

Her hands tied behind her back, Cam couldn't shield her powerful sun charm. She could block Epie's approach, though. Using every ounce of her kick-butt soccer strength, she booted the chunkster in the shins.

Epie's legs gave way and she went down yelping, "She hurt me! She kicked me!"

"Get a grip," Sersee retorted. "Get off your duff, go behind her, and yank the thing off."

Whimpering, Epie obeyed. She slid the sun charm around the chain until it hung on the back of Cam's neck. Then she yanked it. Her startled scream this time was not caused by Cam.

"Ow! Ouch! I got burned!" Epie shook the hand violently, as if she could shake off the searing pain, and dropped the sun charm on the ground. "Help! I need ice!"

Sersee iced her with a frigid stare.

Epie's cries racheted up when she glimpsed her hand. "Aghhh! Look what she did!"

Even Cam was shocked. Burned into the young

witch's palm was the outline of Cam's amulet, as if the heat of the sun itself had branded her. Desperately, Epie pressed her hand against the cold cavern wall and wailed, "She's . . . she's got magick! She's a —"

"Witch?" Sersee mocked. "Of course she's a witch, you dunce."

Cam had no idea how the charm had heated up to burning. Unless . . . Aron's words came to her. *I'll be with you. I've always been with you.* She was inspired. She focused her heat-bearing eyes on Sersee's dark curls. Alex's turban trick had been much too mild. The leader of the perv pack needed a really hot hairdresser.

Wispy at first, smoke soon began to billow from Sersee's long, thick locks. Ooops. Cam had forgotten about Jason. He began to cough, tear, choke . . .

"Want to rethink that?" Sersee said, her eyes burning as much with contained fury as smoke. "Smoke inhalation's a killer, and it doesn't discriminate between wusses and winners."

Cam glanced at Jason, then lowered her powerful eyes. She could turn them on Sersee again, of course, stun and stop the arrogant witch in her tracks. And then run for it. Epie was too freaked to stop her.

Again, there was Jason to consider. She couldn't lug him along. Maybe he'd come out of the spell soon, able to help her? She snuck another peek at him. He slumped, transfixed, against the wall, tears streaming from his stinging eyes, smoke wreathing his black hair. He couldn't even help himself.

Sersee gloated, "Your prince isn't going to rescue you. He's just not himself these days."

Cam growled, "You got what you wanted. Me. Let him go. Whatever you did to him, undo it."

"Don't you even want to know what I did? I'll tell you anyway! It's a little spell I've perfected. I like to call it Robot boyfriend. Composed of all-natural parts — this I assure you," she said with a wink. "He walks, he talks, he chews gum, and best of all, he obeys completely and without question. It's a handy tool, really."

"What part of undo it didn't you understand?" Cam growled.

Sersee put her finger to her chin, pretending to consider the demand. "Oh, what the heck. I'll do it, if only to impress you."

Cam almost exhaled. With Jason on her side, the real Jason, even for a few minutes . . .

"Oh, no, no, no," Sersee scoffed. Taking a sparkling substance from the herb pouch inside her robe, she tossed it at Jason. "I didn't say I'd give you back your boring old boyfriend. There'd be nothing exciting about that. I merely meant I'd return him to the form you saw him in last." She glared at Cam, waiting for her words to sink in. "Hint, hint," she snapped impatiently, brushing the glitter from her hands. "He'll be a real pussycat."

Cam's heart seized. Sersee *had* done the unthinkable.

Shimmering specks began to sink into Jason's skin. Where they'd landed, dark spots appeared.

"Ooo, I love this part." Epie momentarily forgot her own pain in favor of witnessing someone else's.

At Sersee's command, Jason fell to the floor, bellowing in anguish. Cam gasped in horror as his long arms and legs began to shorten, tighten into animal quarters, and the dark blotches on his skin spread, turning into sleek, black fur.

"No!" Cam shrieked.

Jason, writhing on his back, his legs jerking, his feet transforming into sharp-clawed paws, stretched his now thick and gleaming black neck to look at her. For a split second, his eyes locked with hers. "Run!" he roared. Then his cry became a terrified, searing animal scream.

Cam leaped to her feet and tried to lunge at Sersee, but Epie, boiling mad about her burned hand, and probably twice her weight, pushed her back and held her down. Cam felt the heat still coming off the angry girl's palm.

And off Jason's body. He was on the other side of the cavern but his glossy coat was foaming with sweat, his mouth frothing as he snarled and snapped at her.

Jason was a panther now. Completely altered, he paced back and forth before Sersee — waiting, Cam felt sure, for the heartless witch's orders.

"You're torturing him!" Cam tried rushing at Sersee again, but Epie had her pinned. *Don't freak!* It was Alex's voice — but not via T-mail. *Think!*

"He never did anything to you. Why are you doing this?" Cam sounded desperate and she knew it.

Sersee gloated, "You're good at quizzes, or so I hear. Try this one. It's multiple choice: A) Because I can. B) Because I don't like you. C) Because you need to learn a lesson. D) All of the above."

She snapped her fingers and Epie retrieved a studded collar and fastened it around the panther's neck. Shocked and sickened, Cam noticed something she'd missed before. The round orange tag hanging from the collar? Jason's basketball charm.

The charm she'd given him. The sight of it turned Cam's fear to fury. She spat. "Here's my answer. E) None of the above. I don't care why you did this. But you will pay for this."

"How new," Sersee snarled. "Like I haven't heard that before!" The thin witch leaned over to stroke the panther's head.

Cam narrowed her eyes and focused them hard on Epie.

Not fast enough. Sersee jerked up, grabbed Epie by the shoulders, and whirled her around so her back was to Cam. "Can't stun her if she's not looking at you," Sersee reminded Cam. Averting her own violet eyes, she taunted, "You haven't even heard my plan." She licked her lips. "It's just so . . . yummy, so tasty, so . . . romantic. In a twisted sort of way."

"Undo the spell!" Cam tried to sound commanding.

"Too late to reverse the curse this time. Why, what's wrong, Lady DuBaer? You fancy the boy, right?" She slipped a chain around the panther's neck and yanked at it harshly. The animal crouched, its tail switching tensely. "I've found a way for you to be together forever." Sersee reached into her herb pouch again. "Cam and Jason. Together forever. Part of each other, even."

Cam saw bits of the sparkling confetti drifting from Sersee's hand.

"What's she going to be?" Epie wanted to know. "A frog? A snake? Something slimy and ugly, right?"

"Epie, you've let the cat out of the bag." Sersee smirked. "Or, rather, the rat. Rodents," she told Cam, "are tasty tidbits for hungry panthers. And your pet pal is starving."

"Sersee wouldn't let us feed him," Epie explained.

Cam got it. Hit by another wave of nausea, she began to shiver.

"Perfect," Sersee announced. "You're already quivering and quaking like a rat in a trap, and I haven't even recited the spell yet."

"Why do you hate me so much?" Cam asked, frantically hoping to buy time.

"Let me count the ways . . . and whys," Sersee snickered. "You're a DuBaer, born rich and gifted to one of Coventry's ruling families. While I, who will one day rule this island, will have to scheme and fight for it. Everything's been handed to you. And yet you tried to take something away from me —"

Shane, Cam thought.

"Yes, Shane — who has taught me much of the forbidden magick your uncle taught him. Valuable information, to be sure. Why, the transmutation spell alone, the ability to transform a human being into . . . well, pretty much whatever I want it to be, has given me hours and hours of fun."

The vile witch yanked on Jason's collar, and the big cat groaned in pain.

"And just so we're clear," she continued, "know this before you cease to exist. Shane has been playing you. He's not attracted to you, never was. It was all to gain your trust."

"Oh, really?" Cam tore her eyes from the suffering panther. Sersee had accidentally wandered onto *her* turf.

Boys. Cam knew how to fight this battle. She took her shot. "I don't think so. Maybe he taught you to read other people's minds, but he hasn't entrusted his own thoughts to you."

"How would you know?" Sersee fumed. "You can't read anyone's mind!"

"Alex can. Which makes me privy to everything your boy-toy is thinking. Which is . . . he doesn't care about you, Sersee. You're the flavor of the month, a handy toy who helped him when he needed it. He won't be around for long. You're not his equal, you don't have his gifts, and you never will."

"Enough!" Enraged, Sersee flung a handful of glittering herbs at Cam. "Say *adiós,* Apolla," she mocked.

Narrowing her violet eyes, focusing them on Cam, she began to recite: "*Dark magick that poisons the night —*"

Cam tried to break in with the reverse: "*Good magick that sweetens the night —*" she murmured, desperately trying to halt the curse and reverse the spell.

Epie heard her and raced over to clamp a steamy hand over Cam's mouth as Sersee hurried on: "*Dark clouds that cover the light, take this creature as I command. Turn her into a rat, at this hour —*"

Startled by Epie's hand and Sersee's terrifying

words, Cam lagged behind. *Sun that heals us with the light,* she stammered silently.

But it was too late. Sersee was finishing up: "*A rodent the panther will quickly devour!*"

Pain engulfed Cam. Searing, intense. She tried to scream but every muscle in her body, including her throat, tightened, twisting in agony. Her head was shrinking, her face contracting, her belly crumpling in on itself, her legs and arms shriveling as she became smaller and smaller . . .

With her last ounce of human strength, Cam cried out, "Alex! Help! Ileana! Miranda! I'm —"

The rope that bound her fell away and she tumbled to the wet cave floor. She landed, not on her hands and knees, but on paws. Tiny, scrabbling rodent paws.

"Perfect!" Sersee clapped her hands. "I couldn't have chosen a better rodent to tempt a cat. You're a hamster, Apolla — or should I say, a Camster!" She scooped Cam up and brought her over to Jason's snout. Cam tried to speak but could only emit a pitiful squeaking sound.

Sersee was in her glory. "Jason the panther, meet Cam the hamster. No! Jason the panther, *eat* Cam the hamster."

Instinctively, the panther began to drool and snarl. Cam felt his slobber soak her head, drenching a patch of her short, red hamster pelt. Then she was snatched away just as Jason's jaws snapped shut.

Long, sharp fingernails held her. "You'll have to excuse your panther pal's impatience. He hasn't been fed in two days. And where's the fun in watching him slurp down such a teeny, tender morsel?" Sersee asked. "Even if the outcome is a done deal, let's at least make the game challenging."

Although she didn't know if it would come out in English or squealing Hamster-ese, Cam sent one more frantic SOS to Alex, Miranda, and Ileana.

"They can't help you, my little pet, eyes so tiny, red, and scared." Sersee flung her onto the floor. "Miranda and Ileana are powerless. And Alex? Well, normally, I don't gossip, but the scuttlebutt is she's roaming the island. Who knows where she's got to . . ."

"I do," a voice from down the tunnel announced.

CHAPTER NINETEEN
SURVIVAL OF THE FITTEST

It was Michaelina.

Her little hamster heart sinking, Cam dashed across the cold, stone floor, searching for a safe hiding place — and noted that Michaelina was not herself exactly. For one thing, she seemed jittery, and, for another, she was draped in someone else's cape. This one, a vivid burgundy, was way too big for the shortest witch. She looked like she was wearing her daddy's —

Cam didn't finish the thought. She didn't have to. From her vantage point as a lowly rodent, she'd caught sight of something Sersee and Epie could not have seen. Bounding from the floor onto the bench and from there scrabbling into a hamster-sized cranny in the cave wall where Jason couldn't get to her, she watched.

Knowing exactly what was going to happen.

And what she needed to do.

Epie clapped gleefully. "Michaelina!" she called out. "Hurry. You've got to see this. Look what Sers and I did!" At Sersee's glare, she amended, "I mean, Sersee did. But I helped."

Michaelina was still in the shadows. Sersee squinted, tilting her head as if she were trying to figure out why her little lieutenant seemed so nervous and why she was moving so oddly. "How lovely of you to join us," she finally said. "Now haul tush, Mike. We should all be together for this. I've eliminated the problem princess."

As Michaelina stepped out of the shadows and drew nearer, Cam sprang from her hiding place and took a flying leap.

"Arghh! Get it off me! Eeek!"

Eeek? Epie had actually screamed "Eeek"? Cam laughed out loud. Which came out in a high-pitched chatter that sounded as though she'd sucked helium. To create a distraction, she scurried up the chunky girl's leg, bounced onto her fleshy, flailing arms, then ran in dizzying circles around her neck, digging in her tiny claws at every op.

Frantically, Epie tried beating her away, but the sluggish witch was no match for the hasty hamster. Making it worse, the snarling panther was now crouched at Epie's feet, eyeing her hungrily.

Just as she was Cam, though shrunken and fluffy with fur, Jason was probably still himself somewhere under that sleek ebony hide, Cam realized.

Epie's full-volume panic got neither help nor sympathy from Sersee. The formerly fearless Fury was having an "eeek" moment of her own. Michaelina had come out of the shadows. She wasn't alone.

"Company's here!" Alex quipped, emerging from beneath the lush velvet cloak she'd found at LunaSoleil. Aron's cape was more than big enough to cover Michaelina and herself. Back around her neck was the baby quilt Miranda had sewn for her.

Sersee was visibly shaken and momentarily speechless.

"Your thoughts are wildly scrambled, so this is just a guess," Alex continued. "But you seem a little edgy. Could it be because Cam and I are together now?"

"Together — in a manner of . . . well, *squeaking*," Sersee retorted, composing herself. She pointed to the hamster perched on Epie's shoulder. "Honey, I shrunk the witch."

Alex stared openmouthed at . . . Cam? She didn't know whether to laugh — or cry. Then the furry little redhead hanging onto Epie by a claw sent a clear message:

One joke, Cam threatened, *and you're birdseed.*

"You turned her into a small plump creature, perfect prey for a panther." This from Michaelina, fascinated and impressed.

Sersee glared at her. "I'll give you the benefit of the doubt. I'll assume you wouldn't dare betray me, that you allowed yourself to be 'used' by Punk DuBaer only to bring her here, as you should have."

Before Michaelina could respond, Sersee commanded, "Now, snatch the moon charm from around her neck. She won't be needing it."

Michaelina made no move toward Alex.

"Now!" Sersee demanded. "Do it."

Alex folded her arms, confident. "Not so fast, Captain Flash. Your little lackey is under a truth-telling spell. She won't jump when you snap your talons. She'll say and do only what she truly wants to. She told me everything."

"You think?" Sersee shot back, her eyebrows arching dramatically. "Excellent. Then the truth will out, won't it?"

"Watch out! You'll get burned!" Epie shouted a warning. Too late. Michaelina dashed behind Alex and, with one hard, swift pull, yanked off her necklace. The moon charm hit the ground clinking.

Alex whirled on her. "How could you do that?"

The green-eyed witch shrugged. "She told me to. My truth is simple. And flexible. I'm on one side only. Mine."

Alex felt blindsided, betrayed, bummed. Naïve was so not her style. How could Michaelina have played her so slickly that she'd never sensed it?

Sersee snapped orders. "Michaelina, quick! Get the rope and tie her hands behind her back." In one fluid motion, she spun and knocked Cam off Epie's shoulder. "Help her. I need to soak up this moment — before I kill them both."

Keep her talking! I have an idea. The wind knocked out of her, Cam hit the ground scampering and sent a message to Alex, hoping no one would bother to eavesdrop. *Just bait her*, Cam continued urgently, still unsure if her thoughts were coming out in English or Hamster-ese.

English, Alex sent back, then turned and taunted her would-be captor. "Now that you've got me, Skeletor, what are you going to do, frizz my hair?" When Epie and Michaelina giggled, Sersee wheeled on them, silencing them with a glare.

No one noticed Cam skid around behind Alex.

Sersee snorted, "What was that, cactus-head? No, I had a rattier idea. Jason here" — she pointed to the panther, who'd followed Cam's scent and was approaching Alex — "oh, by the way, just so you're clear, I didn't name him Jason. That's the name he came with."

Alex's jaw dropped. Michaelina hadn't mentioned that. But then Alex hadn't thought to ask her.

Sersee continued, "Panthers have greedy appetites. Well, who wouldn't after being starved for two days. He deserves a *double* delicious snack. Besides, how cute would twin hamsters be? Like a Double Whopper?"

Alex felt something tickle the back of her calf, race up her leg, and perch on her arm. Cam.

The panther was now staring up at them, drooling. Keeping a cautious eye on him, Alex blurted, "Watch out, Sersee, there are ferocious spirits in these caves. DuBaer spirits. Our grandfather died here."

The tall, bony witch gloated. "How fitting. We'll just continue the ritual — make dying in these caves a DuBaer tradition! I'll be rid of you forever. The DuBaer do-right twins will never grow to their most bountiful goodness. Pity."

"How could they do that anyway, Sers?" Epie asked, as if she'd just thought of it. "We're unstoppable, isn't that what Furies are?"

"As long we keep our society secret," Michaelina reminded her. "And no one exposes us until we're ready."

Alex was momentarily distracted by a scratchy sound

and something tugging at her rope handcuffs. Correction: gnawing on them. There'd been a hamster in her classroom in elementary school. She'd fed it one day and had gotten bitten. The creatures did have sharp teeth and a fierce bite — sharp and fierce enough to gnaw through rope? Quickly? Alex went with a wild thought. "Does my uncle know about your little secret society?"

"Lord Thantos? Not yet," Sersee said. "But when he realizes all I've done and how puny his nieces' magick is compared to mine, I think he'll take a very special interest in it. In me, in particular. None of them, not one thought I was good enough —"

"Good enough for what?" Alex asked, hoping she could keep the dangerous witch talking, or bragging, until . . . What was taking Cam so long?

"Good enough to be a fledgling, you moron!" Sersee kicked the growling panther away and stomped over to Alex. "To be among the chosen that Karsh anointed each year, to be tutored by the most esteemed Elder on Coventry. Each year, the old fool passed me over. Nor did Lord Thantos regard me as especially talented. He, too, ignored my requests to learn at the hand of a master."

Finally! Alex felt the rope give. She slipped one hand out and, while Sersee continued her rant, reached into her back pocket and gripped the spool of gold chain. Stepping forward, she got in Sersee's face. "Lord

Karsh was right about you. You're not smart enough. You're not good enough. You're not even good at being bad. That's why Thantos didn't want you —"

Mute the baiting! Cam frantically telegraphed Alex, climbing higher on her sister's back. *Just get our necklaces . . .*

I need to put these three out of action first.

"Who are you talking to?" Sersee whirled suddenly. "Where's the rodent?"

"Where's the rope? Is that what you said?" Alex was locked in mock-mode. "It's right here!"

She focused all her fear, rage, and hope, again hearing Aron's words, *"I'll be with you, I always have,"* then willing her father's gold chain to whiz off its spool and whip forward like a gleaming snake, a golden lasso. She sent it flying toward Sersee. It looped through the air at astounding speed.

Not faster than Sersee, however, who ducked.

Fascinated by Alex's telekinetic trick, Epie didn't. She stared at the wildly whipping chain, which slapped her ankles and corkscrewed itself up her bulging body. Like a gold-encrusted mummy, she went down hard.

Recovered from her shock, Sersee lunged at Alex, sneering, "I remember now, you *did* win the telekinesis round. Too bad your aim is off." Gloating, she hadn't noticed the hamster skitter out from behind Alex, didn't realize it was staring at her with smoldering intensity, pinpointing its beady, blazing eyes directly on Sersee's violet orbs . . .

The lunging witch shrieked and froze as Cam's stinging ray blinded her.

Score! She had stunned Sersee. The formerly large-'n-in-charge witch was rooted in place. In the second it took for Cam's beam to completely immobilize her, the First Fury bellowed, "Attack!"

Michaelina made her move. She looked from the chain-wrapped Epie to Sersee, stiff and standing like an angry statue, to the hungry, prowling panther. And she ran, dashing for daylight as fast and as far from them as she could get.

But Jason, starved, taunted, and painfully taught to obey Sersee's commands, crouched lower to the ground, ready to pounce at the twins. Only his eyes betrayed his fear, his abject terror of committing such a heinous act. But his hunger and the cruel instincts Sersee had instilled in him were getting the best of him. Growling, he drooled and bared sharp, flesh-tearing teeth at Alex.

Cam, staring at Sersee from her sister's shoulder, telegraphed Alex: *I'm still myself inside this rodent coat. That means Jason is, too. Talk to him.*

"Jason, it's me, Alex. And this hamster is really Cam. You were right; we were in danger. Now you really *can* help us."

Alex heard or, rather, felt Sersee sending a scrambled message. It must have been something like, "Sink your teeth into them now!" because the panther cocked his head at the frozen witch, his ears up and twitching in concentration.

"Don't listen, Jase. She's evil," Alex pleaded, trying to contain her terror as the animal swung his head toward her.

Jase. Cam's fear began to disintegrate in a wave of aching compassion for Jason. For Jase, whose motives had been pure and unselfish, and whose reward was to be captured, tortured, starved, and turned into an untamed beast, all because of his loving concern for her.

"Jason, I know you're in there somewhere," Alex urgently continued. "You can use your own free will. You do not have to follow her commands. I promise, Cam and I will get you out of this."

The panther's tail began to lash. He bared his teeth at them, his mouth foaming with hunger.

"Kill!" The single cry came from Sersee, who had nearly thawed from Cam's immobilizing glare.

Startled, the panther whirled toward the witch who'd just commanded him — and pounced. As his claws raked Sersee's purple robe, Cam dug her tiny claws into Alex's shoulder. They both watched, horrified as Sersee stumbled backward, her cloak in shreds.

"No!" Alex and Cam screamed together.

Cam's urgency and passion had released her human voice but at a painful price. Her throat burned, her ears rang, and her head ached fiercely. She was nauseatingly dizzy. Violently tightening her grip on her sister, she feared that she might pass out and plummet, smash unconscious onto the rock-hard floor.

"Down, Jason!" Alex yelled, trying to unfasten Cam's nails from her flesh. "Stop. Don't kill her!"

The starving panther started to back off, then changed his mind. He lunged at Sersee, knocking her to the ground, and sunk his teeth into her shoulder.

As Sersee howled in pain and shock, Cam tumbled from Alex's shoulder, landing on the wildcat's back. He swung around roaring.

"No," Alex commanded. "That's Cam!" She grabbed the animal's swishing tail and held on tight. "We don't hurt people! Jason, we believe in healing, helping," she babbled, bouncing along the floor. "So that all things — even Sersee — may grow to their most bountiful goodness."

While Cam clung quiveringly to his back, the panther sank to the floor, exhausted, weak, and confused.

Squatting beside him, Alex put her arms around his slick black neck. "It's okay," she cooed, petting him. "Oh, Jason, we are so sorry."

Cam was down on the cave floor now, breathing hard as she watched Sersee hug her wounded shoulder and whimper. Cam telescoped in on the puncture wound. It wasn't as drastic or deep as she'd feared. Already the dribble of blood was beginning to dry. Jason had been too frail to cause real damage.

"You'll be fine," Alex assured the wounded diva. "There are enough herbs and healers on this island to cure everything."

Okay, Doctor Done-enough, tell her to take two aspirin and call you in the morning, Cam chattered a message. *Remember me? Sister. Twin. Best friend. Hamster! Pick up our amulets, do the unmorphing spell, and get me out of this rat's body.*

Speedily, Alex found their moon and sun charms on the cold, wet floor of the cave where they'd been flung. She held out Cam's sun amulet, expecting her to take it. But raising her paws in exasperation, the little hamster began to babble irritably.

Whoops. Gotcha, Alex sent back, embarrassed. *"Look, Als. No hands. Duh!" Is that what you're trying to say?*

Cam rolled her eyes as Alex held both necklaces,

one in each hand. But the hammered gold charms made to fit together as one whole were not reacting as they usually did. They were not pulling toward each other as if they had a life of their own. They were as cold as the cave floor, not heating to a glowing warmth. Clasping them, looking straight at Cam, Alex began, with a sinking heart, to recite the un-morphing incantation.

I'm not feeling anything, Cam sent nervously.

I know, her sister admitted. *Me, neither. It's not working. No juice.*

Try again, Cam pressed, hoping it wasn't because Alex was trying something alone that they'd always done together. This had to work, she thought, unsure of what other options they had. Ileana and Miranda couldn't help; their powers were sapped. Karsh was gone. Thantos and Idiots, Inc. wouldn't. And Shane? Iffy at best.

The tip of her nose was twitching nervously. Her tiny teeth were chattering. Cam so did not want to leave the cave like this. Equally horrific: If Alex couldn't help her, then they couldn't help Jason.

No! Cam thought — this is *not* how this ends. She was Camryn Barnes, the girl who got what she wanted. She was also Apolla DuBaer — one half of the most promising sister act ever.

Epie was clanking around the floor, struggling with the chains that bound her. Sersee, still nursing her wound, was ignoring them for the moment. Neither would stay that way for long.

I promise, Alex said, though she had no idea how she'd keep it, *we'll figure something out* —

And then she felt it.

Her back pocket was heating up, as if she'd leaned back against a warm oven.

Cautiously, she reached inside and drew out the amulet she'd found in her parents' house, the one Nathaniel had been holding in the portrait at Crailmore, the gold disk with its dancing bear, which she'd planned to give to Ileana.

Cam had not seen it. She had her eyes squeezed shut and was trying to will a vision to come to her. She wanted more than a hazy premonition, a hint, or a clue. She wanted a detailed picture of the future: a visual promise of what was to be.

Alex turned the warm medallion in her hand, afraid to look at Cam in case the charm didn't work. But it continued to heat up in her hand, feeling very much like her moon charm did. As she rotated the amulet, the DuBaer crest glinted in the candlelight, flashing across Cam's stressed hamster face.

Anxiously, Alex began the unmorphing incantation.

All at once, Cam, her face lit by the glimmering

amulet, gasped. And saw herself *as* herself, free of Sersee's curse. Back in her own body!

"*Good magick that lights the night . . .*" Alex recited, holding the disk on which her family crest had been lovingly carved.

"*Moon and stars that make the sky bright . . .*"

She heard her own voice getting stronger as it reverberated off the walls of the cave. "*It is time for Apolla, a good and compassionate witch*

To return to her human form,

To make the switch

From hamster back to Camster, this I request.

To join Artemis and do what she does best —"

Alex stopped for a second. Was there an echo in here? Or was . . . Cam reciting it with her? Was it possible? Cam!

Alex spun toward her sister. On her own two sturdy legs, her face mirroring not just Alex's features but her glowing joy, Cam was back. Their arms reached out at the same moment, their tears dampened each other's shoulders.

"Thank you, thank you," Cam murmured, wondering if she'd really created a vision that had turned to reality.

"Thank Aron," Alex responded, showing her sister

the DuBaer amulet. "This was his. Nathaniel must have left it to him. I found it in the cedar chest."

"Let's use it to bring Jason back," Cam said, stroking the panther's head.

"Let's get out of here first," Alex decided. "We'll take him with us."

"Good plan, twinsies. I bet he'll be thrilled to know you're witches . . . just like us!"

Cam paled. "Oh, no," she murmured.

"Oh, yes," Sersee cackled wickedly.

"Never mind the Queen of Mean," Alex urged, taking Jason's collar.

"Love to hang with ya, Sers, and you, too, Gold-wrapper." Alex grinned at the chain-encased, wriggling Epie. "But you know . . . errands to run, spells to cast, wrongs to right, lives to ruin! Like yours."

Inspired, she handed Cam Jason's leash and whipped the baby blanket from around her own neck. Skullcap, she thought, sniffing the herb-packed panels of the quilt.

"What do you know of skullcap?" Sersee demanded, trying to lift herself with her one good arm.

They ignored her.

Alex clung tightly to their grandfather's amulet. *"Good spirits that dwell within these caves,"* she improvised. *"Ancestors who here went to their graves —"*

She paused and Cam picked up the thread. *"We call*

upon the heritage that is ours . . . to put these Furies to sleep . . ."

Alex shrugged. *"For hours and hours?"*

"Good enough!" They each drew a pinch of skull-cap from the quilt and together let it rain down on The Furies.

CHAPTER TWENTY
A BUMPY ENDING

Cam and Alex dashed back through the twisting tunnels of the enormous caverns, the panther at their heels. They'd reached the slippery steps leading up to LunaSoleil's basement when Alex flung her arm out, blocking Cam.

"What do you hear?" Cam asked.

"Someone's . . . wait, no, there are two of them," Alex replied. A huge grin spontaneously erupted on her face just as the trapdoor above them flew open.

Hovering at the top of the steps were their beloved guardian and the woman they were just beginning to know but already loved. Ileana and Miranda.

Startled gasps gave way to a torrent of questions, answers, expressions of joy and relief — all tangled up, since everyone spoke at once.

Neither Miranda nor Ileana had actually heard Cam's anguished cries for help, but both women sensed that the twins were in trouble. Ileana rejected her witchy senses, still not trusting her instincts.

Miranda trusted them completely.

She'd run from Crailmore, found Ileana, and together, the women made a beeline for LunaSoleil.

Miranda put a consoling arm around Cam, studying her daughter, who had all the symptoms of having been transmutated. Her eyes were glassy, her skin sickly pallid, her hands shook pitifully. What had she become and who had cursed her? Involuntarily, Miranda shuddered.

Apolla and Artemis — her babies, hers and Aron's, had been forced to tread on very dangerous ground. They'd been exposed to powerful, dark magick that no one their age, especially the uninitiated, should have gone through. The twins were out of their league. Worse they might not be able to save themselves the next time around. She wanted them to stay, but Miranda knew they had to go back to the mainland, their best chance of staying safe.

She was about to tell them when she was interrupted by Ileana, who'd knelt down to study the panther. "I see you managed to adopt a pet while all this was going on."

Before Cam could explain, Alex jumped in, a mischievous twinkle in her eye. "He's not exactly a pet." She deliberately turned to Miranda. "Uh, Mom . . . Cam would like you to meet her boyfriend."

Cam elbowed her with more force than necessary.

Which led Alex to rub her arm and giggle, "Bad hamster!"

Miranda was stumped. Ileana lifted her clear gray eyes to Cam and said gently, "They did this to a friend of yours?"

"We didn't have time to un-morph him. We'll do it now." Cam took Alex's hand and clasped her sun charm.

Ileana leaped to her feet. "Bad plan!" she announced.

"Huh?" Now the twins were stumped.

"Before you show off," their guardian witch said, "think for a moment. Together, you have the ability to return your friend to his proper form —"

"We have to," Cam interrupted, her voice catching. "They used him; they hurt him."

Miranda understood now. "The moment he takes his true form, he will remember everything. He'll have questions, of course. It's your choice, Apolla. Are you ready for that?"

Cam wasn't. In her eagerness to make Jason whole and human again, she hadn't considered the side effects. "So what do we do?" Her stomach twisted at the possibility. "We can't leave him —"

"Speaking in *your* native tongue — *duh!*" Ileana rolled her eyes. "No one is suggesting that. Sit down, my brave, foolish fledglings." She softened, hearing Karsh's voice in her head, then reached for Miranda. "Come. You and I may be weathering a 'power outage,' but there's much we can teach them."

Miranda hesitated. "What you're about to teach them is well above their level: tracker skills. We probably —"

"They're quite advanced, I assure you," Ileana explained. "I say we go for it."

"Let's," Miranda decided, a little of her own rebellious nature coming back. She liked the feeling.

And so, under the guidance of the women they trusted and loved, Cam and Alex repeated the incantation that brought Jason back painlessly to his human form. While he groggily shook his arms and stretched his neck, they learned a spell to wipe out memory. With oil of valerian root, which Miranda contributed, and a foggy green crystal from Ileana's herb pouch, the twins chanted the incantation. And Jason, blinking at Cam as if trying to bring her into focus, seemed to fall asleep. Lastly, they cast the transporting spell to return him to his friends and what was left of the vacation he should have been enjoying.

Back at Ileana's, Cam and Alex got ready to go. Miranda and Ileana were in the front room waiting to escort them to the ferry.

While Miranda looked on with amusement, Ileana lugged her furniture back to where she'd had it before Cam's restless reorganizing fit.

"When I need a decorator," their stylish guardian grumbled, "I'll send for Emily Barnes. Of course," she quickly tagged on, "I appreciate everything you did here, especially the cleanup. That was a real gift."

"Speaking of —" Alex began.

"— we have another gift for you," Cam finished.

Ileana, who normally adored gifts, was somehow ill at ease. "What for?" she cracked. "My generous hospitality?"

Cam clarified, "Just for being our cousin."

Alex opened her hand. The DuBaer family crest sparkled, glinting in the late afternoon sun. "Welcome — officially! — to the family."

"Strange as it may be!" Cam added.

Ileana's hand flew to her lips; her electric gray eyes widened. She turned away so no one would see them grow misty.

When she turned back, Miranda had cupped Cam's face with one hand, Alex's with the other. "This, Artemis and Apolla, is what I'm proudest of. The talent, the power you were born with. But the kindness, the selflessness, and the compassion; this is a gift no one can give you. Use it well."

The four women set out for the ferry — Alex in her frayed denim jacket hoisting her backpack; Cam, back in cargoes, wheeling her rollie — each buried in her own thoughts.

Cam was disappointed and blamed herself for all that had happened. Jason would forget all this. She wouldn't. She'd caused him unbearable torment. Worse, she'd fallen for Shane, a deceiving skeve. A liar. With Jason, what you saw was what you got. It was all right out there.

"Sis," Alex busted into her head. "Try this. How about, with Jason, what you see is what you *want* to see. Maybe the boy has layers, depth, secrets you don't want to see."

"Thanks, Oprah," Cam cracked.

The "normal" girl from Marble Bay had arrived here feeling like a stranger in a strange land. Like ET, an alien who only wanted to go home. Instead, a part of her finally admitted what Alex seemed to have embraced from the start. They had two homes. The one they were going back to and the one to which they would surely return. Two halves of her heart that made a whole. Like herself and Alex.

The twin uprooted from Montana had arrived here and connected immediately. But Coventry was not exactly the paradise she'd thought it would be. This island of witches and warlocks, its history, its people, its magick held frightening secrets. Only some were buried underground. She and Cam had been sent away long ago because the island wasn't safe. What Alex now knew was that Coventry might never be safe for them.

Coventry would remain a mystery. Like Shane. Like Michaelina. Like why the truth-inducer spell didn't work on her.

"Are you sure of that?" Ileana had tapped into her brain.

When Alex explained, Ileana pooh-poohed her. "Rubbish! You got that right out of my spell book. Of course it worked."

"I thought so, too, at first," Alex protested. "She seemed to be spilling everything. Then she betrayed me. How do I know which was the true Michaelina?"

Miranda softly said, "Maybe they both are. Listen to me. No one is just one way, one-dimensional. Not even your uncle Thantos, though you might like to think so. Like anyone else, a witch can be confused, unsure of what and who she really believes. You ordered her to tell the truth — perhaps she did. In Michaelina's mind, she may have been merely exploring her options.

"The first one that appealed to her, that spoke to the rebel in her, was most likely Sersee. Then she met you. My guess is the two of you captivated her, piqued her interest, and probably got her to question her loyalty. It's a start —"

The thought popped into Alex's head so unbidden and so quickly she couldn't squash it. *For a certified wacko, Mom's pretty smart!*

"I HEARD that!" Miranda put her hands on her hips and pretended to be angry. She wasn't very good at pretending.

Which sent all four witches into a major fit of giggles followed by the tightest, longest, most loving group hug ever.

"All's aboard that's goin' aboard!" Forgetting for a moment where they were, the quartet looked up, startled, as the ferry pulled up to the dock, its captain covered with bruises.

"That happen often to you?" asked Alex, pointing at the welts on his arms, although she knew the answer.

"Whaddaya, some kinda witch doctor? Happens all the time," he groused. "My last run of the day, some witch put a spell on the lake, messed my vessel around. I got bounced, nearly capsized."

Hence the nickname Bump. The flabby Cap was used to bumping around his boat like a pinball, courtesy, Cam guessed, of The Furies and other mischievous sprites on the island.

"S'why I don't spend any more time around here than I need to. No, sir." Then Bump bellowed, "Didja hear me? All ya witches, get on yer broomsticks and move it."

Never prouder to be witches, Cam and Alex — the T'Witches, born Apolla and Artemis — did just that.

Ileana walked Miranda back to Crailmore, turning down the invitation to come inside. She had no interest in seeing Daddy Dearest or hearing his warped version of history, particularly his lies about Karsh and Nathaniel's friendship.

The beloved trickster wasn't here to refute the hulking tracker. Well, Ileana thought with a toss of her luminous blond locks, Lord Karsh Antayus might no longer be alive, but his memories, his truth, lived on in his precious journal. He'd bequeathed it to her, Ileana, the daughter he'd never had but reared with all his wisdom and love.

And all he'd asked of her was to be generous of heart, to read the pages he'd written for her, to share them with Cam and Alex, and to keep the girls safe so that they might fulfill their destiny.

Limited powers or not, nothing would stop Ileana from granting his last request.

Nothing!

Except this: When she arrived at Karsh's cottage, and went to retire the precious journal, it was not where she'd left it.

It was gone.

ABOUT THE AUTHORS

H.B. Gilmour is the author of numerous best-selling books for adults and young readers, including the *Clueless* movie novelization and series; *Pretty in Pink,* a University of Iowa Best Book for Young Readers; and *Godzilla,* a Nickelodeon Kids Choice nominee. She also cowrote the award-winning screenplay *Tag.*

H.B. lives in upstate New York with her husband, John Johann, and their misunderstood dog, Fred, one of the family's five pit bulls, three cats, two snakes (a boa constrictor and a python), and five extremely bright, animal-loving children.

Randi Reisfeld has written many best-sellers, such as the *Clueless* series (which she wrote with H.B.); the *Moesha* series; and biographies of Prince William, New Kids on the Block, and Hanson. Her Scholastic paperback *Got Issues Much?* was named an ALA Best Book for Reluctant Readers in 1999.

Randi has always been fascinated with the randomness of life . . . About how any of our lives can simply "turn on a dime" and instantly (snap!) be forever changed. About the power each one of us has deep inside, if only we knew how to access it. About how any of us would react if, out of the blue, we came face-to-face with our exact double.

From those random fascinations, T*Witches was born.

Oh, and BTW: She has no twin (that she knows of) but an extremely cool family and cadre of bffs to whom she is totally devoted.

MEET THE T○WITCHES

Camryn Barnes—Smart, upbeat, and popular, Cam is best of breed all around. Except for one bone-chilling secret: Cam sees things happening before they happen. Very bad things.

Alexandra Fielding—Spunky, punky, and sarcastic, Alex is all about making it from day to day. Life's tough, but Alex deals. Except for the weirdness. Alex hears things. The things people think but haven't said.

HAVE YOU READ ALL THE BOOKS IN THE
T☉WITCHES SERIES?

T☉WITCHES #1: *THE POWER OF TWO*

Identical twins. Separated at birth. For one very good reason . . .

If they ever met, they could combine their powerful gifts and help people, maybe even save a life. They could figure out who they really are and who their parents really are — or were. And they could fall into very evil hands. Guess what? They're about to meet.

T☉WITCHES #2: *BUILDING A MYSTERY*

Alex and Cam finally learn some secrets about their past. But they still have a lot to uncover. Fortunately, there's new eye candy in town to keep the girls' minds off their troubles. Cade is dark and beautiful and seems to have secrets of his own. Alex is lured in . . . and it takes both girls to break his spell. But are they strong enough to hold back the evil that surrounds them?

⊙WITCHES #3: *SEEING IS DECEIVING*

Cam's and Alex's powers are getting in sync, and the twins can't help themselves. They're reading people's minds, using magick on the soccer field. It's bringing them closer together. But it's forcing Cam and her bff, Beth, apart.

When Alex sneaks out to an all-night party, she suddenly finds Beth — and herself — in terrible danger. Thantos, the evil one who wants the twins eliminated, has taken Beth hostage. Must Alex sacrifice herself to save her sister and her friend?

⊙WITCHES #4: *DEAD WRONG*

Alex's skeevy stepdad has resurfaced . . . and he wants Alex back. Like, for good. And Evan, Alex's Montana bud, is crashing. He needs help, stat. Time to 180 to Alex's hometown.

But there's more trouble in Montana than the twins ever expected. The powerful warlock Thantos has followed Cam and Alex. And he has a present for them. One that's six feet under.

T☺WITCHES #5: *DON'T THINK TWICE*

Cam's best, Bree, is unraveling, and Cam feels locked out. Not so for Alex, who has been breaking into people's minds. She knows all Bree's secrets. But before the twins can help Bree, she is taken away. To a private place, for serious help.

There, Bree meets a mysterious woman who is able to heal her like no one else. But this woman is more than a stranger. She holds the key to everything that Cam and Alex have been searching for. If only they can get to her.

T☺WITCHES #6: *DOUBLE JEOPARDY*

Miranda. The mother Cam and Alex never knew they had. A magnificent witch from the most powerful family on Coventry Island.

Rewind.

Locked away in a sanitarium the twins' whole lives, Miranda is broken. Physically and spiritually. And her freedom comes with a price. Cam and Alex will have to part with something that means more to them than they ever imagined.

And for once, their guardians can't help them.